The Six Mile Inn

To Linda:
All my best. I
hope you'll enjoy this.

[signature]

What follows is a work of fiction based on actual events. Some of the
book's characters and events are real. Others are products of the author's
imagination and used fictitiously. Any resemblance to persons and events,
living and dead, is entirely coincidental.

Visit www.booksurge.com to order additional copies.

The Six Mile Inn

A Novel

Lee Martin

2009

The Six Mile Inn

ACKNOWLEDGEMENTS

Grateful acknowledgements to my former boss, Bob Dandridge, Colonel, Ret., USAF, and his wife Faye for their gracious Southern hospitality and a tour of the city; to the Reverend Jim Crutchfield and his wife Judy for biblical content and their Christian example; and to the kind and noble people of Charleston.

And to Lavinia. . .for the story.

FOREWORD

There were those who said they saw her even decades later, flitting through the narrow alleys or along the ballast stone near the battery. Some claimed that as they passed the iron-gated courtyards on Meeting, the once faintly scented Confederate Jasmine took on the sweet, intoxicating aroma of her lilac water. And still others swore they caught a glimpse of her, wearing the white gown with the boulle sleeves and high lace neck upon the road along the Ashley, searching frantically, hopelessly for her lovely inn beneath the riven oaks. But within the millisecond it took for the eyes to blink, she would be gone, leaving behind only the moonlit moss that hung from gothic branches like an ancient crone's gray hair.

For nearly two centuries now she has ruled the night. She is the ethereal phantom who roams the Carolina low country. Her name has been on the tongue of every child who dares to repeat her story at the risk of experiencing glissando chills and the accompanying prickly bumps. For generations her story continues to be handed down to children and grandchildren alike, compromised and embellished along the way until it is now nearly impossible to separate fact from fiction. But there is one thing for sure: her spirit lives on, somewhere, whether trapped within the walls of the Old Jail or in the woods off the Old Dorchester Road. And until this world releases her, Hell continues its wait.

On the morning after, the bell at St. Michael's bonged seven times to usher in the light of that winter's day in 1820

Charleston. Slow-rising smoke billowed from the chimneys of homes and kitchen houses, filling the orange horizon with a lazy gray haze and making the morning air seem all the colder. A lone figure stood at the foot of a mound of freshly planted South Carolina soil at the rear of the Unitarian Cemetery, far from any other grave. The Georgian dressed in a long black overcoat and sag-brim hat pulled the coat even tighter into his chest in response to the raw-bone temperature on that February morning. Or perhaps he was just reacting to the sudden chill that entered his spine while he digested the events that led to this day, the day he would finally be leaving Charleston.

The sonorous peal of the huge bell never failed to remind the older town folk of the events a half-century before and how vulnerable a society can be. During the Revolutionary War, the British had stolen away the church's very soul when they lifted down the bell, shipped it across the Atlantic to England with the intention of melting it down to make just one of the many cannons that would be used to kill Americans. However, it was ultimately recovered and returned to the people of Charleston intact. To these citizens and the man at the gravesite, the toll of the bell on that day celebrated a triumph of justice and the extermination of evil.

The frozen earth smelled pungently dank, further turning the Georgian's stomach. If not for his vigilance and keen sense of hearing, perhaps this grave, or one close by, may well have been his. He drew in a deep breath, then exhaled, taking note of the vapor spewing from his mouth into the frosty air to remind himself he was still alive. Over his right shoulder, the sun lighting up the eastern sky was the welcomed friend that he would never again take for granted. Nothing would ever again have a sense of urgency in his life, as he would savor each day and thank God Almighty for even the smallest of blessings.

A low fog had settled over the churchyard giving him the impression that a congregation of spirits had seeped out of their crypts and were carrying on about their newest neighbor. Certainly, the spirit of the one buried not six, but twelve feet beneath the mound, was in Hell, and could not ever return to this world, as promised, to torment those responsible for her demise. Her words had rung out over the crowd less than twenty hours before, attaching themselves to his dreams during the night, and awakening him out of a cold sweat.

It was important that he be there that morning to see if the earth had been disturbed. He and other curious on-lookers had witnessed the burial somewhere around three the day before. The gravediggers had to reinforce the pit with planks in order to reach the twelve-foot depth to keep the earth from caving in on them. The body was buried face down so that if the eyes ever opened, they would look in the direction of Hell. Furthermore, the spirit would never be able to rise, but only sink lower into the fiery abyss that Satan had prepared for her.

The man took from his pocket a can of fine Virginia tobacco and poured it into a folded cigarette paper, sealing it with his tongue. The smell of sulfur from the match head struck off the heel of his boot prompted him to say aloud "Well, missy, I reckon you're smellin' much the same thing about now." Drawing the tobacco into his lungs, he found his nerves had quickly settled. But after smoking only half of the tobacco, finding it strangely distasteful and bitter, he dropped it onto the mound and contemptuously mashed it into the soil with the toe of his boot.

The sudden chortle of his mare tied at the wrought-iron gate startled him, but gave him notice it was time to go. Taking one last reassuring look at the fresh grave and before turning his back on his would-be assailant, he whispered "May you *never* rest in peace."

After the War of 1812 had ended, an influx of rogues and renegades descended on the city, creating unusually perilous times for many low-country South Carolinians. Wagoneers hauling cotton, tobacco and pecans bound for the north and west were often set upon along the highways just beyond the Ashley. Piracy and 'patriot privateering' abounded in the near waters just off the Charleston peninsula as well. Merchant ships leaving the city docks sailed scarcely ten miles from port before they fell into the tentacles of Captain George Clark with his motley band of Whites, Blacks and Hispanics.

Charleston, an early walled city of the British Colony, was named for its king, Charles I. By the early 19th Century it was easily the largest city south of Philadelphia, rich in cultural diversity and the indisputable capital of the antebellum South. It was the peoples of Europe, Africa and the Caribbean who shaped the city. Planters and merchants descending on the city a century before built opulent houses of Georgian, Palladian and Federal Greek Revival architecture with large verandas overlooking English gardens and courtyards.

Belying the city's beauty, urban blight lay on its outskirts. Rows of shanty houses and lean-tos sprang up as quickly as mansion homes were erected in the city's heart. Clearly half of the city's population were the non-citizen blacks, comprised of about eleven thousand slaves, the Mulatto elite and free Africans. Most of them spoke Gullah, a dialect derivative of African, Portuguese and English. White aristocrats conducted business with the light-skinned Mulattos, protecting both them and their businesses, yet maintaining their social distance. Although the Mulattos had gained wealth, respect and status in the community, the darker ones along with free black men were sometimes snatched off the street to be sold into slavery by enterprising whites. The law made little effort to see the slave traders prosecuted, which infuriated African groups such as the Brown Fellowship Society and the Free Dark Men of Color.

It was Denmark Vesey, who along with Gullah Jack, struck fear into the hearts of many Charlestonians, attacking and killing slave traders, merchants and civic leaders alike. After vengeful citizens had burned several black churches in retaliation, word reached the streets that Vesey and his band were in turn conspiring to burn the entire city to the ground. But Vesey was elusive and his reign of terror would last a full four years before he was finally corralled and positioned under the hangman's noose.

In the year 1819, Charleston had endured an epidemic of yellow fever, seen several important century-old buildings go up in flames and was graced by a visit from President Monroe. And it was on the 18th of February of that year a band of notorious robbers and murderers was rounded up north of the city, forcing an end to their decade long vocation of crime. Among them was a woman from the Charleston Neck region, beautiful yet deadly as a coral snake, an eloquent quoter of Robert Burns, yet a spouter of venomous profanity.

CHAPTER ONE

On a fall evening in 1818, James Addison, a middle-aged Charleston silversmith, spurred his horse from a gentle trot into a full gallop on the Old Dorchester Road as it narrowed into a heavy forest of Live Oak trees. Huge fifty-foot long branches clothed in Resurrection fern joined above his head took on the appearance of a moss-draped canopy, further darkening his way. Addison was returning from his daughter's wedding in Goose Creek and as he had gotten a late start on the afternoon, he had wanted to be well past this point on the road before now. It was a perfect place for an ambush. Just the week before, his friend, Jonathan Brown, had been severely beaten and robbed of $140 by two masked horsemen that had ridden upon him near the fork at Ashley Ferry just ahead.

Bringing his musket up from the saddle and training it in the direction where the robbers had assailed Brown, he brought his mount up to racehorse pace. Through the dark portion of the road, past the Ferry trail, the rider exited the danger area, catching sight of the lovely inn just off to his right at the end of a lane. As the gelding was now snorting and panting, Addison reined him in to a walk. Now, well beyond the shadowy oaks and with only a tree or two on either side of the road, he felt relieved. The last rays of the setting sun steamed along the road behind him and glistened red off the sweaty shanks of the gelding. Addison slid the rifle back into its sheath, removed his hat and dabbed his forehead with a handkerchief. Even at six thirty on a mid-October afternoon it was still rather warm.

"That's far enough, friend!" the voice rang out from his left. A large white horse supporting a masked rider suddenly appeared from behind a clump of scrub-brush. Startled, Addison nearly fell off the gelding, but managed to recover and pull his musket partially from the sheath.

"Leave it," barked the voice behind the mask, "or I will put a very nasty hole between your eyes." The muzzle of the highwayman's rifle was now no further than five feet from Addison's head.

"What is your business with me, sir?" asked Addison, redundantly.

"Such a foolish question from a man staring into a mask and a gun. I'll trouble you for your purse now." The robber's voice was firm, almost playful. He wore a black, wide-brimmed hat, turned down in all directions and a makeshift mask made of burlap covered his entire face. Two shagged, but largely rounded holes were cut in the cloth, fully revealing the man's piercing black pupils.

Addison raised his hands even without command to do so. "I….I don't have much, mister. Maybe thirty dollars."

"That'll do. I'll also take that watch and bob on your pants as well. Quickly! Toss 'em here."

Obediently, Addison pulled both coin and currency from his pocket, then unhooked the bob from a belt loop and held them out. The robber made a clicking noise with his mouth to move his horse forward and then he snatched the booty from Addison's hand.

"Now be off with you. Do not look back or follow me. If you do so, your family will not even find your bones. Now *go!*"

Addison did not need further prodding. Digging his spurs into the gelding's hide, he commanded "Yow!" and accelerated into a gallop. Even above the rhythmic thunder of hooves, he was still able to hear the pounding of his heart in his eardrums. Visibly shaken and glad to escape with his life, Addison reached the city proper in less than a half-hour. He needed a whisky, badly, and decided to stop at Chartwell's Tavern before reporting the matter to the constables.

Around the scarred oak table sat four men, gulping down the volatile spirits, which not long after soaking their intestines would cross the blood-brain barriers. As the rum and whisky flowed, the dialogue became slurred and often unintelligible.

"If the law will not act to bring these blaggarts to justice, then we will do the job *for* them." David Ross brought his glass down forcefully on the table and wiped his mouth with a sleeve.

"Hear! Hear!" two tablemates echoed.

"In just the last two months at least a dozen wagoners and city merchants have been ambushed and robbed up on Dorchester. Some even killed," continued Ross. "I am convinced that the very vermin that occupy the Five and Six Mile Houses are in some way connected, if not in fact the perpetrators themselves."

Addison poured a second glass of rye to gain control of his nerves. "Didn't Six Mile House used to be in your family, Ross?"

"That's a bitter pill for me, Addison. My father built that place more'n thirty years ago, but the Fisher woman's old man stole the house from him."

"How so?"

"The man was a card shark. A cheat, if you will. Pure and simple. It was the year of eighty-seven and there was a poker game right in this very establishment." Ross took another swig from his glass and stared at it with melancholy eyes. "My father was down to his last dollar, but in holdin' four of a kind, he knew no one could beat that hand. So he put up the deed to our

LEE MARTIN

house against a pot of about $400. The cheat came up with a straight flush. I'll never forget my mother's face when my father came home and told us we didn't live there anymore. The bloke allowed us to gather only enough belongings to fill our wagon." Ross turned up his glass, then sent it crashing into the bar. "My old man hung himself the next day. By God, he killed himself over a goddam card game. One day, my boys, one day I'll get that place back."

For a while the men at the table said nothing. Then a man named Carter spoke up. "Let's take out that gang at first light. We'll get Fletcher and Finch to go along. They're the best shots around. Maybe with five or six more we can flush 'em all out."

"In due time, my friend. There will be an opportunity one day soon, and I will be pleased to lead that posse."

Once known as the Benjamin Ross estate, off the Old Dorchester Road near the ferry on the Ashley just north of Charleston, and nestled deep among massive, moss-adorned oaks, stood the stately old board-and-batten house. The porch was of the long and wide veranda type at the foot of which grew trumpet vines that spiraled around the banisters and columns. On the front of the house were eight-paned windows flanked by the black shutters that had last been closed during the hurricane of '04. The only casualty from the storm was the roof, which after thirty years of age was in dire need of repair, anyway.

Several inns had popped up along Old Dorchester over the years, some named rather uncreatively for their locations in proximity to the city of Charleston. First there was Four Mile House, then Five Mile. But neither of these was as charming and inviting as Six Mile House. The reputation of them all was at best, sordid. Although there was gambling, drinking and other illicit goings-on, Six Mile House had been known more so for

4

its hospitality, good food and liquor, and for the beautiful proprietress known as Lavinia.

Six Mile House, sometimes called the Six Mile Inn, had been built in 1785. In '91 when Washington came to Charleston, there was great speculation about where he would stay, and the new proprietors of the house campaigned along with other inn owners in Charleston proper to attract the president. But Mr. Washington stayed with his friend, Dubose Heyward, even though it was his intention to stay in public accommodations. He wrote:

"...I have determined to pursue in my Southern visit not to incommode any private family by taking up quarters with them during my journey...".

Since Six Mile House was neither upon the traveled roadway that led to the new Ashley Bridge nor located in the city, the boarding house was considerably less frequented. Unless one were traveling in from Georgia or down the Goose Creek Road and saw the sign, it would just appear as another rustic, two-story private residence off the beaten path. Just to the north and east, a few hundred feet away, was the Collinwood Plantation where brick one-room slave cabins with dirt floors inhabited by slave families stood adjacent to the mansion house. Raggedy black children might be seen scampering about, while the adult Africans appeared at the end of the day as though the very life had been beaten from them. Realizing there was no hope, they would be doomed indefinitely to lives of servitude and degradation.

Lavinia Fisher felt for these people, but knew there was no way she could help or befriend them, else face the ire of Master Collinwood and the authorities for interfering into a man's business. She often found herself challenging the local and federal governments over many issues, not just slavery. She and her husband, John, owners of the inn for the past seven years, had been taxed to the hilt, not to mention having to pay the toll across the Ashley on their trips for supplies into Charleston two or three times per week. She hated all politicians, especially the leering, lecherous swine of a man, Chauncey Harriman, the city magistrate. Lavinia's opinionated nature did not go unnoticed by the authorities and Charleston folk alike, and it certainly did not win her any friends.

On a Tuesday morning in the late summer of 1818, Lavinia whisked about her kitchen room as husband John sat groggily with both hands wrapped around his warm porcelain coffee cup. She had taken him well into the morning hours into a surreal world of frenzied bliss with her body, tearing into him like a ravenous dog on a piece of meat. Yet she had sprung from her bed before seven to prepare him the hearty breakfast to which he had become accustomed after a night of fiery passion.

"More?"

John nodded and pushed his cup across the table toward her. For the third time from her mother's Wentworth tea service she poured out a hot stream of the rich Bolivian blend. They exchanged intimate smiles and knowing glances without word. Lavinia's face was pink and amazingly refreshed. Her eyes still had the glow of romance left over from the hours before. The faint fragrance of her exotic bath oil remained, teasing his nostrils beyond the aroma of his coffee. His smile suddenly broke into a laugh and he shook his head.

"What's so funny?" she asked.

John sucked in another sip and wiped the bottom of his moustache with a cloth. "His face. The look on his face."

"Which look?" she asked. "His look of perfect lust when I leaned into him to serve his tea? Or the look just after his wick went out?"

"He was indeed well taken with your bosom, my dear. I expect if your breasts had fallen out of your brassiere, his eyeballs would have popped clean out of their sockets." John laughed again. "They all are set to wonder what precious jewels lie beneath your clothes. If they only knew what I know."

She swatted his cheek playfully with a spatula. "It is not only our male guests who wonder such things. Half the men of Charleston would love to know as well."

It was this last comment that brought a frown to John's rawboned face. His mouth drew taut under the wide moustache. The men of Charleston. A sore subject with him. There was not one among them he did not despise. When it came to Lavinia, they were lechers all. And as many were well educated and affluent, they treated him like the dung they scraped from the bottom of their boots.

After the robust coffee had fully revived his senses, he pulled from his breast pocket a fresh Dominican, bit off an end and struck a match to it. A few puffs to get it started, he expelled a long, satisfying stream of blue-white smoke. Placing his hands behind his head, he leaned his chair back on its two rear legs. Yes indeed, most of the city bastards had dull, ordinary lives and were married to fat and ugly women. He was married to the most beautiful woman in Charleston County and because she was his, he was richer than the lot. Let them ogle her all they want.

His mind returned to the events of last evening. "Guess the rats are havin' *their* breakfast about now."

Lavinia kicked a leg of John's chair, causing him to return it quickly to all fours. "The cows will not milk themselves and the mare needs her breakfast, Mr. Fisher."

"Yeah," he said. "S'pose we'd better get up there."

John followed Lavinia down the steps of the veranda and up the slight grade to the west side of the house toward the barn. Dew from the tall grass around the flagstone transferred chlorophyll onto the lace fringe of her petticoat, staining it a lime green. The early morning rays of the sun captured the radiance of her alabaster skin and she tilted her head slightly toward the fiery ball, closing her eyes and parting her lips as if to drink in its warmth.

As she entered the barn, Lavinia stopped to stare at its northeast corner where there lay new, fresh hay. The pause had become a daily ritual of sort, always prompting a tear, but lasting only moments until she took the deep, healing breath that restored her morning purpose. Still, after all this time, the pain remained. She would always assure there was hay in place to cover the spot where precious blood ran nearly twenty years before.

John went directly into the barn to retrieve the horse that drew their carriage, and began to groom the beautiful roan with a stiff brush. Lavinia stood by the rail fence, taking account of her handsome rake of a husband who barely more than a hundred fifty pounds still cut a dash in his wide-brimmed hat and black, well-groomed mustache. She walked up behind him, put her cool hands around his sides and onto his rippled abdomen, then slipped them inside the buttons of his shirt to stroke his dark chest hair. Her touch compelled him to stop the brushing and he placed his rugged hands onto hers, closing his eyes as if in some sensuous stupor. She was often the temptress, using her hand like a wand, causing his adrenaline to surge and every systolic, diastolic beat to be ever so pronounced. As wild as John had been and as recalcitrant as he had become, Lavinia knew how to rein him in as though she were stopping a team of spirited horses dead in their tracks. Under her spell, any man would surely lose his senses.

The bray of their seventeen year-old albino mule in the lush meadow beyond the barn summoned them to the fence rail where John propped up a muddy boot. The mule seemed irritated having to share his space with the old bull. The *cantankerous* old bull. From his pocket John took the remnant of his half-smoked cigar, struck a match to it again, then took a few short puffs to get it going. "I will have to cut that ol' boy up one of these days. Reckon eatin'that beef would be like gnawing on shoe leather."

"I should draw the milk", Lavinia said. "The cows have that 'pleading' look in their eyes. There is much for both of us to do today, John Fisher. Remember, you are to pick up my gingham at the mercantile when you go in for supplies. Now get back to it!"

That was Lavinia. She could be the loving, sensual partner one moment and the demanding nag the next. Such an enigma, she was. As she hustled back to the barn, John flicked his stogie into the wet grass and proceeded to brush down the mare. The morning breeze blew toward them the sweet aroma of jasmine that engulfed much of the fence rail, helping to balance out the perpetually-pungent stench of manure and piss.

Only moments later both John and Lavinia turned their ear toward the road in response to the clopping echo of horse hooves. John caught the first sight of the handsome figure in black, already now walking past the large gateposts toward the front of the house below.

"Spruce yourself, Lavinia. It is your beau, the parson. And I am sure that he could not sleep last night in anticipation of seeing you first thing this morning."

"Oh, John. Your jealousy will one day be the end of you. You know his only intentions are to have my fine fanny sitting in one of his pews."

John turned his attention back to the mare so as to further ignore the presence of the visitor and mumbled "It's just unnatural for such a man, surely approaching forty-five, to have never taken a bride, parson or not. He ain't a priest, so what's he all about? I'm sure he's had intentions on you these years, otherwise I should question whether he has a preference for the men."

Lavinia cracked him hard on buttocks with her hand. It obviously hurt her more than him. As the pain rang all the way up her arm, she composed herself, brushed back her shimmering raven hair with her fingertips, then gave John a wicked half-smile. "Don't go on so much about him, John. He is a righteous man who has always treated me respectfully. Now put on her welcome face and go with me to greet him."

Matthew Cowher, the associate pastor in the Second Independent Unitarian Church under the Reverend Anthony Forster, was indeed a handsome, slightly graying man, always casting kind eyes and a warm, reassuring smile. He was but a young minister about twenty-five when he first met eight year-old Lavinia. For the past nineteen or so years, he had tried to take Lavinia under his spiritual wings, stopping by from time-to-time to talk to her about her soul, the Good Lord, and occasionally partake of her hearty meal of pintos, onions and cornbread. John, although always showing a reluctant cordiality, did not hide his jealousy well. If he and Lavinia had any discord, it was usually over this man. Actually, this went for any man who was overly friendly or caught leering at her flawless beauty.

Matthew had broken from the Unitarian Universalists and their practice of 'free religion.' He had bantered over the years with religious liberals who refused to accept the deity of Jesus Christ, but nonetheless was given authority by Forster to minister to a separate Unitarian Christian congregation at a later hour on Sundays. It was a small group of parishioners, but rather than join the Baptists or Presbyterians, the Christians chose to remain loyal to their family tradition and history as members of the church.

As Matthew did not find the Fishers inside, he leaned against the columned portico and looked out to the east toward the line of glorious oaks and riven pecan trees, a few of which had been split by lightning, and all of which impeded his view of the Ashley. The huge oaks resembled gnarly, prehistoric creatures with sprawling tentacles of roots growing above ground. Under one of these trees, not fifty meters from the house, lay the small graveyard where rested the bones of Lavinia's parents, older brother and aunt. The flat, simplistic gravestones had already weathered to a point where the names were nearly indiscernible.

Her parents had come to America from Ireland in 1781, shortly after Cornwallis' surrender to Washington at Yorktown. They had first settled in Charleston, joining the feudal aristocracy of the South Carolina low country. After her father had fallen into some luck in a tavern poker game, he and his wife moved the six miles north on the river to start up the newly acquired inn. Lavinia was eight in 1799 when renegade Indians from the Creek Nation raided the inn, massacring both of her parents and thirteen year-old brother, Winslow. Her father took an arrow in the throat and when her mother went to his assistance, she was decapitated by the knife of a brave. Winslow had taken Lavinia up to the barn and covered her with hay. When he was not able to fully conceal himself, one of the braves found him and gutted the boy with all four prongs of a pitchfork he had located by the door. A cavalry troop that had been chasing the renegades, swiftly descended on the braves, first killing them by musket fire, then hanging their bodies from the oaks to the Epicurean delight of ravenous vultures and crows.

After the massacre, the Reverend Cowher took in the child Lavinia, providing consolation and spiritual witness while setting her up in his housekeeper's care. The only surviving relative of Lavinia's family was her mother's sister, Fiona, who within six months came from Ireland to administer to the child and take over management of the inn. As all hope for life and love had been buried beneath the outstretched arms of the oaks, Lavinia grew up under the stern raising and tutelage of her aunt. Together, they carried on the business of the inn, taking in temporary boarders and travelers for a dollar a day plus meals.

Matthew was also at her side to comfort her ten years later after her Aunt Fiona suddenly keeled out of the front porch rocker from an apparent heart attack while sipping her evening tea. Her funeral was officiated by the Reverend Forster at the Unitarian Church. Eighteen year old Lavinia sat in the first pew alone with only a handful of church members behind her. The old woman had made no friends, so this accounted for only the dozen or so women who came to the funeral, largely out of commitment to their church.

Even so, only two or three of them had a word of condolence for Lavinia. She was after all just an orphaned child who lived in a boarding house in the countryside. And she was not one of theirs.

Jesus' stained glass image stared down at Lavinia with kind yet condemning eyes, compelling her to turn her face away. Her aunt had not taken her to church more than a month of Sundays in the ten years and this did not give the child much opportunity to learn about Jesus. Anyway, what had He done for her?

As the Reverend Forster strained to deliver his rather generic eulogy about a woman he did not know, Lavinia placed her eyes on the handsome face of Matthew Cowher sitting in an ornate Russian oak chair behind the pulpit. Occasionally, his eyes met hers and somehow she knew his look was not one of pity or sympathy. They were wanton, embarrassed eyes, eyes that had been found out.

She had heard none of the minister's words. Her mind was far beyond the message, returning to those early years of innocence when Matthew and his assistant had taken her in. His counsel had been instructive yet loving. She remembered the touch of his hand and the many nights hence that she had lain in her bed still feeling that touch as though he had never released it. And again just before the funeral when he passed by the pew, he touched her again, allowing his thumb to lightly stroke her hand. It was a different touch this time, even sensuous. Though thirty-five, he still looked twenty-five. Why did age have to matter, anyway? But she supposed it did matter to him and to the fine citizens of Charleston.

Reverend Forster offered a prayer, but Lavinia's eyes remained open, staring at the coffin. She had no tears for the old woman. Aunt Fiona was nothing but a hateful intruder into Lavinia's life, an opportunist who took full advantage of family tragedy to better her own self in life. Lavinia hated the fact that in a few hours Fiona would be laid to rest along side her beloved family under the same Live Oak.

She did not hear the *amen* nor did she notice that Matthew had descended the altar and positioned himself beside her. His hand once again caressed hers. It was a firm hand yet gentle. He helped her to her feet and she began to play the thespian's role so well. She allowed her body to sway and swoon just a little so that he would steady her with a strong arm about her waist. The eyes of the dozen women silently gossiped to one another.

Lavinia had only known loneliness throughout her young years. After the aunt's passing, Matthew who had himself been lonely and had certainly cultivated feelings for the lovely Lavinia, failed to act on them. He was not sure how his parishioners would react to his taking on a wife of eighteen, when he was already thirty-five. Moreover, for some unknown reason, it appeared many of the Charlestonian women had rejected Lavinia. Maybe it was because she did not grow up in Charleston society in a family of affluence and fine breeding. Or perhaps there was a stigma associated with orphans as being uneducated, uncultured and just plain unfortunate. But he had grown to love the teen and there was still enough time to debate the pros and cons. After all, she had no suitors and if he would wait until she was in her twenties, then the age difference should not matter so much.

Lavinia stayed on as mistress of Six Mile House, taking on boarders and overnighters, cooking their breakfasts and dinners, and providing them with a comfortable room, clean sheets, a bathtub, and an evening of her lovely company complete with hot tea and ginger cookies. Only a year after her aunt's death, Lavinia took in an itinerant Georgian who had come to Charleston to work on the docks. John Fisher was a dashing sort with dark, piercing eyes and a square, handsome jaw. As he was both feckless and charming, she was immediately attracted to him, allowing him to stay long after the five dollars for five nights' stay was gone. John, also struck by her passionate, imperious blue eyes and raven hair, saw a fire in her that suited his nature well. As he had once preferred the frail gentility of aristocratic teens he had courted in Savannah, Lavinia's nonpareil beauty and unbridled personality fancied his heart like magnolias in their summer bloom.

Within days, John and Lavinia began to carry on a torrid love affair, and in scarcely three weeks they were married by a local justice. Matthew was crushed, as he had waited too long to approach her. He had fallen victim to his own stupid procrastination based on what was a false assumption that his church would not accept her. For weeks on end he endured fits of depression and despair, until three elders, sensing his melancholy, chided him with stern words of warning.

Now, nearly nine years later, Matthew stood on the porch of the woman whom he had loved but lost to a heathen and a rake. If he could not save her from the ills of the world, he would work to save her soul. Matthew knew this would be a battle, for the blackguard to whom she was married had the devil in him, and when the devil lives in your house, he will surely dwell in your heart.

Matthew finally caught sight of the couple at the barn and gave them a wave. Finding the large rocker comfortable, he settled back to take in the beauty of the land. Off the porch to his left was Lavinia's arbor on which grew abundant vines of succulent Catawba grapes. Near the gateposts were two large Rose of Sharon bushes, boasting beautiful pink blooms. On the distant hill just to the near side of the pasture where a six-month-old colt frolicked in the morning sun, a chorus of wildflowers harmonized in an interlude of stunning reds, yellows and whites. The lady's touch could be seen all over, complementing God's own handiwork. But they would all too soon fall victim to the first killing frost.

As the Fishers descended the bank and traversed the flagstone, John made it a point to place his hand in Lavinia's so that the minister would take notice.

"Good morn, Matthew", she called to him, prompting him to shed his hat and bow ever so slightly.

"Lavinia, how the sun makes you the more radiant." He caught John's glare. "What has it been....two months? I usually see you bounding along the Charleston streets especially down Meeting near the church, but not lately."

"I have missed seeing you as well, Matthew, but matters at the inn have prevented me from more frequent trips. Normally John runs all my errands." Her deep blue eyes set upon his and Matthew's heart did not know whether to be saddened or filled. He remained on the porch by the door as the Fishers made their way up the steps.

"Would you have a drink to quench your thirst, parson?" John asked. "Perhaps a glass of ale or a shot of whiskey."

Lavinia turned full-faced to John. The flirtatious eyes she had for Matthew had now turned icy and venomous. Their lethal silence nearly knocked her husband aback. He did not say another word, but gave Matthew a sheepish parting nod and turned on heel back down the porch steps toward the barn to prepare the roan for the morning's travel.

When John was far from sight and ear, the sun in Lavinia's face returned from behind advancing storm clouds. She managed a sweet smile. "Sit with me on the porch, Matthew. I will make you some cold lemonade."

"That would be delightful. When you return, I will ask you to share a devotion with me."

Lavinia did not want Matthew to see the reluctance in her face, so she turned away quickly and went into the house. She would rather have just talked about old times or what was going on in town, but she had so enjoyed his company and counsel over the years, that she would resign herself to anything that came from his mouth. As she loved John more than herself, she had also loved Matthew, maybe since the first time she saw this handsome Irishman, but knew she could never bring him down.

He was too righteous a man for her and she could never train her heart to believe in the spiritual things that were his very life's blood. And she could never have fully loved a man who was too good for her.

Only moments after John had passed by the stately gateposts on the mare, touching the brim of his hat to the minister, again without word, Lavinia came out onto the porch carrying a tray with a pitcher of drink and three glasses. She caught the last glimpse of her husband disappearing from view through the moss-draped branches of the oaks toward the Old Dorchester Road. "I thought he would drink a glass of ade before he rode out," she said, continuing with her lingering gaze. Then she snapped her head in Matthew's direction as though John was suddenly history. She gave Matthew a glass and filled it with the tart, pulp-filled liquid.

Matthew gulped two swallows as mannerly as he could, given his parched throat, and settled back into the rocker. "I think John does not like me much, but trust that he does not perceive me as a threat to his marriage. I would surely not say or do anything that would make him ill at ease."

"Oh, don't mind John," she laughed. "He's a protective sort. If it walks on two legs and shows me the slightest attention, his bowels are in an uproar. Normally, he just sulks and mopes around, but gets over it in a day or two."

Matthew took more swallows of his drink and sighed. "That, my dear, is excellent. Tart, yet sweet. It alone was worth the trip out here."

"Why did you come by, Matthew? Surely not to just lead me in a devotion." She took a delicate sip from her glass, then placed her attentive eyes on his.

Matthew looked away so that his eyes would not betray him. He wanted so much to tell her how he had longed for her those years that she had given to John. Matthew had purposely stayed away these weeks as she had come to him in his dreams, and his dreams had haunted his consciousness during the day. So often he had committed adultery with her in his heart and to him, that was the blackest of sins. He had prayed daily that God would forgive him. He really didn't know why he had come.... whether it was to see her or to square off against his fear and shame, having it out with the devil once and for all.

"Perhaps I shouldn't be here, Lavinia. But I *would* like to share the Word of the Lord with you. I have sensed over the years that you have been so much in need of something spiritual in your life, but have shied away from it. You could easily go toward the Light, you know, yet you seem afraid and even appear callused at the idea."

"I am not sure what you mean, Matthew." But she did know.

"There are only two paths before us, Lavinia. The path that beckons us to walk in the Light or that path that leads us to darkness."

"You speak in riddles. I am not that educated as you know, but I have read the Bible and find it allegorical and confusing, just like you."

"I will let the scriptures explain it to you." He opened his weathered and frayed Bible and after flipping through several pages with a wetted finger, lines of serious reverence formed in his forehead. "Let me begin with verse five, Chapter One of First John. *'This then is the message which we have heard of Him, and declare unto you, that God is light, and in Him, is no darkness at all. If we say that we have fellowship with Him, and walk in darkness, we lie, and do not the truth. But if we walk in the light, as He is in the light, we have fellowship one with another, and the blood of Jesus Christ, His Son, cleanseth us from all sin.'"*

Lavinia took her eyes off Matthew and placed them back onto the road where John had earlier departed. Softly, she said "You don't know me, Matthew, nor what is in my heart. The color of my heart is black and it belongs in the dark. This 'light' of yours is not for me, so you may as well give up on saving my soul. It can never be saved."

Matthew formed a frown between his eyes. "It grieves me to hear you say that. We are never so lost that God cannot open His door so that we may find Him. Do not allow the tragedy that has befallen you in your life to consume you. God has only challenged you with difficulties so that you may draw near to Him. I fear for your soul, and don't want you to be exiled after this life to eternal damnation."

"Spare your fear, parson, for *I* am the owner of my soul."

"No, Lavinia, your soul belongs to God. If you do not freely give it to Him, even you will lose it."

"Matthew, I have only condoned you to talk about your God because I have loved you for these many years. Please, for the value of my love and admiration for you, let me be."

His eyes widened and lips parted. Did she mean love in the romantic sense or like something she would feel for her father?

"Yes, it's true, Matthew. You were always there for me….. when my parents and brother were killed, then when my auntie died…." She stopped short and looked down at the folded hands in her lap. "I have done things, if you must know. Terrible things that would make you despise me, never wanting to see me again." She looked up again into his eyes and said softly "I am not afraid of the darkness. In fact, I am comfortable there. That is why I could never be more than your friend, and can never set foot in your church. Yes, I did hear your sermons as a child, and they put that light in me, Sunday after Sunday. But my darling Matthew, the flame would not stay lit, for as you preached to me, a sinful young girl, I was imagining what it would be like to be with you in bed, and even to be your wife. The light, you say? You were the light to me."

He was catatonic and had not even realized the glass had slipped from his hand onto the porch. "Lavinia, I..." He actually had no words to finish his thought.

Sensing his uneasiness, she placed her hand on his and softened her voice to a near hush. "Your 'light' will never find me, Matthew, nor I it."

After a few moments of silence, then realizing his glass had fallen and rolled to the edge of the porch, Matthew slowly retrieved it. "I'm sorry," he said quietly. "I spilled the lemonade."

"It's all right," Lavinia said softly and formed her hands partly around the glass and his large, strong fingers. She leaned in close to his face and pasted her eyes on his. Yes, John was a pleasing, even torrid lover. But she somehow knew Matthew would be a good lover as well. He would give her tender, companionate love. A love that would make her *feel* loved and not just ravaged.

He could have swept her up and kissed those velvet, pink lips, but knew such a foolish not to mention sinful notion would be perhaps as much out of pity than love. He shook it all from his head like a dog shakes out a head full of fleas. In the midst of his temptation remained pious constraint. "I.....had no idea, Lavinia. You shouldn't have told me all this. Why did you wait after all these years? Why not even ten years ago, before..."

"Before John."

"Yes."

She looked away and an unholy amount of time seemed to pass before she spoke again. "It is well that you should go," she said.

He nodded, then took her small hand into both of his and kissed it.

Lavinia turned abruptly without further word and went into the house. The man whom she deeply loved slowly mounted his horse, then slapped the reins onto the nape of its neck. As he rode away, she watched him through the dining room window. His form blurred through her misty eyes. She hated herself for crying, but she knew she could not see him again, as he was indeed a threat to her love for John. John had good reason to be jealous. As she had the power to bewitch all men, Matthew would surely have lost his faith over her. Anyway, if she had ended up with Matthew and spoiled this good man before God, much as a rotten apple does another, God would surely strike her dead.

As she put aside the tray and pitcher, she picked up Matthew's glass and kissed the rim where his lips had been. "Goodbye, Matthew. Goodbye, from my heart. And do not tread on it again."

Scarcely had Matthew departed when Lavinia heard the hoof-clops of another rider approaching from the opposite direction.

CHAPTER TWO

Colonel Nathaniel Green Cleary, looking every bit the Irishman with his wavy red hair and granite jaw, sat at his mahogany desk occasionally dipping the quill pen into the well, then scratching his name onto official documents that lay before him. Again he signed......"*August 15 in the year of our Lord, 1819. Nathaniel Cleary, Sheriff and Chief of Constables.*" At forty-two, he was the spitting image of one of his two heroes, Thomas Jefferson. Old Hickory, Andrew Jackson, was the other. If Cleary had lived in Virginia, specifically the Charlottesville or Richmond areas, he may well have been mistaken for the third U.S. President. Of course, that would have been thirty years prior, as Jefferson was now well into his seventies. Cleary, a former colonel in Jackson's Army, was a laconic man of quiet authority who carried himself with great dignity and military bearing. Known also for his integrity, emboldened eyes and pleasant demeanor, he was endeared throughout the city, with or without his badge.

Cleary had been wounded in battle in his left side by fragments of grapeshot. The round had partially clanged off the muzzle of a cannon and shattered the lower ribcage, leaving him in perpetual pain. His malady had by no means diminished his erect posture and stately gait, as he was able to climb the steps of the courthouse or saunter along the city streets at a brisk pace. Head high and polished to the bone, he always tipped his French tricorn hat to the ladies and carried himself with the dignity of the refined and cultured gentleman that he was.

The colonel had commanded a dragoon brigade of Freemen of Color under the charismatic Andrew Jackson in the Battle of

New Orleans. Henri Favrot, then the mayor of Charleston, and whose son served as one of Cleary's lieutenants in early 1815, learned from his son of Cleary's heroics in battle. Cleary had led two counterattacks from the defense of his position that thwarted an overwhelming British assault. More important to Favrot, Cleary had fired his pistol into the brain of a Redcoat who was standing over Favrot's son, cocked and poised to thrust his bayonet into the young lieutenant. Shortly after the war when Cleary resigned his commission to return home to Charleston, the mayor insisted Cleary assume the newly vacated position of Chief of Police.

In office for just over four years, Cleary had arrested the very worst of mankind, many of whom had the misfortune of occupying the Old Jail on Magazine Street. Built in 1802, it was a huge brick and mortar facility that resembled an 18th Century Bastille complete with fortified gates and iron-glass windows. Dank, filthy and dungeonesque, it compelled a newspaper reporter to comment that the jail "satisfies everyone who feels a jail should look like a jail". Most of the ground floor cells had straw-strewn dirt floors accommodating mostly vagrant gutter rats. On occasion, one of Charleston's lower-life women would find herself involuntarily boarded at the penal establishment, but she was afforded one of three cells on the ground level that actually had a stone or oak plank floor and a bed. The jail stood on a tract of land that had once been a public burial ground. On either side of the jail were miserable houses occupied by miserable people. Directly across the street was the Sugar House which held Negroes convicted of minor offenses. In later years it became a 'poor house' which was sometimes occupied by sick and wounded sailors. They, along with the indigent, earned their board and medical care by manufacturing coffins for the city.

Cleary had overseen the hanging of slaves from the Great Rebellion, murderous pirates haunting the Atlantic coast, and sailors whose drunken back alley brawls had left many a victim with his life's blood spilling into the cobblestone streets.

There were twenty-four thousand citizens in Charleston in 1819, mostly law-abiding and requiring as few as eight constables who were stationed along the dock and throughout the rows of seamy bars. After two years of splendid service Cleary was re-elected, accruing more than eighty-five percent of the vote. He was indeed held in high esteem by constituents and politicians alike, with one exception. Chauncey Harriman.

The Harriman and Cleary running feud was the constant buzz of the city. As forthright and respectable as was Cleary, the magistrate, Harriman, was evenly despicable. Unfortunately, the lewd and obnoxious Harriman was appointed to his post by the South Carolina Supreme Court and could be removed only by the court. Upon seeing him, women quickly crossed to the opposite side of the street to avoid the portly man's leer and suggestive greeting. There were rumors about sixteen-year-old whores he took to his bed, even within earshot of his invalid wife, and complaints from young, beautiful society women he accosted and groped in social gatherings.

Cleary had both approached and warned Harriman about his lewdness and the use of his power and office to position himself above the law. The magistrate only scoffed and retorted with threats that the Chief could not only lose his job, but perhaps he might find himself carved up by the wharf crew and fed to the sharks. One such barb drew the Irish out of Cleary and he pinned the magistrate to the wall with one large hand, choking off the man's wind just below the Adam's apple. As three constables pulled the Chief away, Chauncey's gurgling voice could be heard echoing throughout Market Street. "I will have your badge for this, you son-of-a-bitch!" But Cleary was in such high regard by Charleston that Harriman would not dare try having him removed, else face certain civic unrest. After the altercation, both Cleary and Harriman went out of their way to steer clear of one another. In fact, each learned the other's routine to assure their paths would not cross on any given day, except if a case compelled Cleary to appear in the magistrate's courtroom.

Lavinia opened the front door to secure a better view of the approaching rider. He looked to be a paunchy, well-dressed and fairly affluent man in his upper fifties mounted on a large black horse around sixteen or seventeen hands high. She immediately felt more at ease. As the inn was a hundred meters off the Old Dorchester, occasional rogues or beggars filtered into Six Mile, giving her cause for fear, especially when John wasn't around. But over the stone fireplace rested a musket that John had taught her to load and fire and she would have no qualms about igniting a mini-ball and propelling it into the forehead of a would-be robber or molester.

"Hello in there!" the man called. When Lavinia stepped out onto the porch, he added, "The name is Hastings, madam, William Hastings. Have you a room for the evening?"

"Yes, of course, Mr. Hastings. My name is Lavinia Fisher. I have three such rooms for your selection. The fare is one dollar for the bed and one additional dollar for dinner this evening and breakfast on the morrow."

"Perfect, madam. It is madam, isn't it? The place has the look of a man about."

"Yes. My husband, John, and I are the inn's proprietors. Please come in and enjoy the comforts of our house. I have baked ginger cookies and can serve you fruit as well to tide you over until dinner."

"Wonderful, Mrs. Fisher. I have been traveling since well before dawn and having begun my trip in Philadelphia many days ago, I felt I could go no further. By the bye, how far is Charleston from here? It is difficult to tell from my map." Hastings dismounted, secured his bedroll and purse, and made his way up the porch steps.

"Why sir, you are only a few miles from the city. If you had ridden less than an hour, you would be crossing the bridge into Charleston."

"Well then, I am glad that I gave out here. Your inn is most inviting and such a splendid setting approaching the river. Perhaps I wouldn't have felt as comfortable in the city. Yes, I will be fine here." Hastings allowed Lavinia to enter the house first and then stepped into the hallway. He took account of the finely polished pine flooring, the wainscoted walls, the upper half which boasted a delicate rose print paper, and a painting of what appeared to be lush-green Irish hills dotted with craggy stone.

"Please make yourself comfortable in the parlor while I get you the cookies and some lemonade. We do have a small bar set up off the kitchen. If you prefer a stronger drink, I will get you a tankard of ale." Lavinia waited for his response and noticed that he had already settled into a wingback chair, jamming his purse between an over-sized leg and the chair's arm.

"Since it is still the morning, I would be pleased to sample your lemonade, but may partake of some of your fine Southern bourbon later in the day."

As Lavinia readied the ginger cookies and strawberries, Hastings clutched at his purse and stretched out deeper in the wingback, propping his boots onto an ottoman. When she came out of the kitchen into the parlor with tray in hand, she found Hastings slack-jaw in nearly a supine position, snoring loudly to a point where it was difficult to count the eleven chimes of the grandmother clock.

John returned just after three and Hastings was still asleep in the very position he was in when he lost consciousness. The sound of John's boots scraping dried mud onto the doormat awakened the man. He first grabbed for his purse, then rose unsteadily to his feet to acknowledge John's entrance. Hastings, a very large man about six feet four and out-weighing John by probably seventy-five pounds, looked down at the smaller man and extended his hand. "You must be the Lady Fisher's husband. I am pleased to make your acquaintance."

John appeared surprised to see the stranger and replied "John's the name, and who might you be?"

"William Hastings from Philadelphia, sir. I happened upon your sign and this charming house on my way to Charleston, and it seems I will board with you this evening...and perhaps next."

"You are welcome, Mr. Hastings. What business brings you this way, if I am not too bold?"

"Not at all, sir. I own a livery business and am in need of another coach. Perhaps the finest builder of coaches is right here in Charleston, and I have contracted with the Farthmore Coach Works to purchase a Stafford carriage, complete with gaslights and leather seating. I will meet with him on the morrow and then select a horse from the Middleton Stables before returning here."

"Good" said John. "Lavinia and I will provide for your comfort as long as you wish to stay. You must also partake of her wonderful blend of hot tea this evening before you retire."

Lavinia entered the parlor at that moment to hear John's invitation and added "You are welcome to walk about the area as well, especially down to the river. I will have dinner for you at six."

"It won't be none too soon, ma'am." The very mention of dinner caused his stomach juices to gurgle.

At five-thirty Hastings returned from his walk and made his way along the narrow, creaking hallway to his room where he splashed water from the basin on his dresser onto his face. The image of the fifty-seven-year-old man in the mirror looked back at him with a face that was drawn and tired. It was a rather distinguished face just the same. He missed his wife and adult children these long days on the road, but after tomorrow's business, he would see them again in a week or so.

As he looked about the guestroom, he could see the lady's touch everywhere. It was a quaint room, meticulously papered with an eye-appealing floral pattern in red, blue and gold. Ruffled curtains of Federal blue accented the walls very nicely and a matching spread garnished the wrought-iron bed that had obviously been handcrafted by a master blacksmith. A bouquet of deep red roses lay on the dresser and a basket of fresh gardenias had been placed on the floor near the footboard of the bed. Still, the room's sweet fragrance seemed to do little to camouflage a peculiar odor that permeated throughout.

Hastings settled in at the dining table and as he waited for his dinner, he took account of the large room that continued into the parlor. It was homey with ten-foot ceilings accented with carefully-carved crown molding over green and gold wallpaper, all tastefully done. A tilted mirror just above the musket over the slave-laid stone fireplace made the room appear larger than it was. Lavinia's fine English china, hand-painted in a type of Asian theme depicting houses with turned-up roofs and bonsai trees, graced the table. A silver tea service, embossed with squiggly carvings that once may have belonged to an English aristocrat and brought to America two dozen years before, was the table's centerpiece.

The dinner was indeed succulent: salt pork and pintos, fresh corn and greens, then strawberry-rhubarb pie for dessert. Not only was this woman beautiful, perhaps the loveliest creature he had ever seen, but she was a masterful cook as well. Having his fill after double helpings, she offered him another glass of ale, and he retired to the veranda to draw in the fresh evening air. It was exuberant. Though the breeze off the river offered up a hint of fish, it was soon overtaken by the intoxicating perfume of gardenias blooming at the foot of the porch.

Hastings had napped nearly four hours that afternoon and he was far from being sleepy. The only discomfort he had was a bloatedness from the heavy dinner and he was compelled to belch a few times to relieve the gas. At around nine the sky had darkened. The palmetto branches silhouetted against the rising full moon gave the haunting image of a windmill's blades. It was a most lovely early fall evening for William Hastings. He could enjoy a rural Southern setting such as this in his waning years, that is if his wife were not so much ingrained in the Philadelphia social scene. Perhaps one day he would sell his business and consider a place like Charleston. His wife would surely fit in with Charleston society. Yes, it was indeed lovely country.

In a few minutes Lavinia appeared on the porch, bringing Hastings a hot cup of her spiced tea. The idea of anything else put in his stomach summoned nausea. But not wishing to insult the graciousness of his hostess, he reluctantly accepted. Perhaps it would cap off the restful afternoon and scrumptious meal.

Hastings sat for another half hour sipping the tea until it was gone and until the cool breeze ushered off the river served to perk his suddenly groggy brain. He had nearly fallen asleep again and the time was nigh to turn in. Tomorrow would be an important day, as he would take the five hundred dollars that lay at the bottom of his purse beside him and purchase the carriage and horse that would complement his business.

When he rose from the veranda rocker, he began to feel somewhat dizzy and nauseous. Teetering across the porch to the doorway, he told himself he had nothing to drink but the ale after dinner, so perhaps there was something he ate that may not have agreed with him. Grabbing pieces of furniture to steady himself as he stumbled through the parlor, he bounced off both sides of the walls along the hallway. He fumbled with the knob and flung open the door to his room. In his clumsiness, he swung the door wide, allowing it to bang against the wall and then slam shut. He worried that he was making too much noise and would alarm his hosts.

Hastings had intended to relax at the secretary before retiring to pen a letter to his wife and enjoy the ambiance of the room. But too drained to carry himself further, he secured his purse under the pillow and plopped onto the spread without disrobing. The severe nausea in his stomach developed into excruciating pain. He lay on the side of his face, still, staring at the petals of a soft red rose in the wallpaper, much like the roses on the dresser and those that his wife grew in their back yard. Hastings suddenly clutched his chest and closed his eyes tightly in wincing pain. The eyes then relaxed, opened for a moment, then half-closed. The grandmother clock in the parlor chimed ten bells when he breathed his last.

About half an hour later, outside of the boarder's room the floor creaked with two sets of footsteps. Lavinia and John paused at the door to listen for activity. The light from the still burning lantern was visible through the crack between the door and floor. She knocked lightly on the door, then called out "Mister Hastings!" No reply. The proprietors looked at one other, then turned the knob slowly to open the door.

The man lay sprawled cattycorner on the bed with one booted leg hanging off the side, the toe barely touching the floor. "He looks done for," remarked John. "I'll check him to be sure."

John went to the bed and kicked Hastings' boot, receiving no response or reflex. Taking the tips of his fingers and applying them to the cool skin near the jugular, he felt no pulse. John then turned toward Lavinia and smiled. "Such power, my dear, you have wreaked from your pot of special tea, that you could stop a man's heart from beating. You must feel like a god."

Lavinia put her small hand onto his and gave it a squeeze. "Let's see what we have earned ourselves tonight." She jerked the pillow from beneath the dead man's head, turning the limp skull slightly to a new position on the bed, then snatched the black purse from under the head rail. She gasped as she pulled out the currency and then let out a small shriek that sounded like a bird. Dancing gleefully around the room, she exclaimed, "There must be over five hundred dollars here. We did well indeed this night. As he told us he was to buy that magnificent carriage from Farthmore, I think I would be more fashionable than he atop the seat of that fine leather."

"If that's what you will do with the money, then so be it, my sweet." With that, John tucked the spread into the mattress and reached between the bed and wall for a lever. He pulled the lever down and dropped one side of the bed that was bolted to the floor, spilling the body of William Hastings into the cellar and onto an earthen grave of lye. The bed hung from the hinges perpendicular to the pine floor, exposing the large rectangular hole cut into the floor, until John reached down to pull it back to its upright position. Hastings was whisked away and the room restored in less than a minute. The lye would facilitate the body's rapid decomposition much the same as it had those beneath Hastings who had over the years met their untimely demises as well.

Lavinia re-straightened the covers as though she were preparing the bed for the next guest, like a cheerful maid on a Saturday morning sprucing. She then took John's hand and led him up to their bedroom, where she allowed him to unlace the breast area of her soft blue georgette garment and drop it to the floor. Lavinia had become John's teacher, both in murder and in bed. She kissed him passionately with soft, succulent lips as he slipped his hands inside her French silk pantaloons. She breathed heavily and moaned, then sucked harder on his lips and strapped her bare legs around his back. Dropping her gently onto the bed, he thrust himself into her. The thrill of ending life ignited a fiery passion in both of them as they enjoyed each other's body. While making love, they talked wickedly about the night's adventure... and their profit.

CHAPTER THREE

The morning sun spilled radiantly into the room, promising another fine day of warm weather. The Fishers were usually up before dawn for breakfast and to feed the livestock, but Lavinia had been a tigress the night before, compelling John to summon her juices on three occasions. Both she and John were well spent and their bodies had soaked up over eight hours of blissful sleep. Even after nine years of marriage she drove John Fisher to near madness with the insatiable passion that boiled between her legs. She could be a clawing, ravenous wildcat in the bedroom, but yet paradoxically, while gliding along the streets of Charleston, give off an aura that exuded a kind of purity.

The sun's rays blinked open John's eyes as he felt a tickling on his chest hair. Lavinia who had been awake for a while was looking at him, gently running her hand over his upper torso. Her touch made his mouth turn up at either end under the normally well-groomed handlebar as he broke into a mischievous grin. His face was handsomely chiseled. The jaw line was strong and his cheeks, slightly recessed. Deep vertical creases outlined the edges of his mustache that made him look older than his twenty-eight years. It gave him a raw, roguish look that Lavinia loved. But underneath that rugged exterior was a weak spirit whose outward masculinity was betrayed by an unempowered, timid nature. Lavinia was his match head. When she ignited, it was only then that his heart caught fire. But then when it came to murder, it was obvious he would never be able to end a life himself.

When Lavinia finished milking the cow, she stepped out of the barn and set the heavy bucket down in the sandy clay. Below, lay Six Mile House, majestic and proud, a little in need of paint, but strong and stately, just like her. A vision of the dead Mister Hastings lying twisted in his bed crept into her mind, but as always, she repelled these images as they tended to taint the counterfeit portrait of sanctity and tranquility she associated with Six Mile House. She shook from her head the memory of the night before, except the booty she captured and so well deserved for having to take such drastic measures against Hastings. He certainly wasn't going to give it up graciously.

Lavinia stooped to retrieve the heavy bucket of milk and proceeded back toward the house. Matthew's God had surely blessed her with a perfect day. The humidity was low as the rich blue sky exploded with cauliflower clouds over the palmettos and magnolias leading to the Ashley. She stopped at the back porch, set the bucket down, and gathered up the garden knife that lay in a pot on the back step. Carefully clasping a thorny branch of the rambler rose bush with her finger tips, she snipped off several of the stems that had climbed out of control, some as high as six feet on the trelliswork. She was so like the rose, beautiful and velvety. But get too close and she could cut you in a hundred different ways. She would spill your blood like the thorns that lay beneath that blanket of beauty.

Placing the roses in a clear vase in the parlor, Lavinia stopped to drink in their intoxicating aroma one more time before readying herself to go into the city with John. He was still up in the barn, taking an inordinate amount of time to hitch the roan to their buggy. She stepped back out to the rear porch to call him. The ire in her voice ripped the morning air, having no trouble carrying into the barn.

"I'll be there in a farthing, Lavinia!" he shouted back. Finishing the hitch, he angrily slapped the reins on the hindquarters of the mare, causing it to lunge forward and step on his boot toe. John winced and muttered "Gawd, must everything be on that woman's time-table?" Eventually, but with delayed purpose, he drove the buggy down the slight grade across the flagstone to the side of the house and parked it at the gatepost.

"It is about time, John Fisher. Do you not sit and think of ways to bring out my Irish? You know we have business in the city. I wish to take our gains to the bank before the sun sets on us. Now make haste and preen yourself so that I will not be ashamed to accompany you on the street!" The eyes were piercing when she showed her impatience.

Lavinia found herself more frequently angry with John these days. Being the jealous and paranoid personality he was did not set well with her, and then true to form, John assumed her moodiness was because she had Matthew Cowher on her mind. He knew she idolized the minister, noticing that she was different around Matthew than she was in the company of any other man. As Lavinia proved her love for John night after night in their bed, he knew her mind and he knew her eyes. Although in their moments of passion she told John she loved him, her blank, straightaway eyes told him that Cowher was in her head. Perhaps she envisioned that it was he whom she wished were in her arms. John knew that if he ever had the backbone to kill a man himself, the first would be Matthew Cowher. It wasn't that he despised the minister, but if Cowher did live inside Lavinia's head, cutting the man's life short would erase him from her mind. John kept his tongue, however, saying little to her about the parson. He knew anger lived behind those beautiful eyes; but the eyes and the tongue could turn deadly in an instance, striking like a Samurai's sword, slicing him up, piece by piece.

Charleston, with its hide-bound, liberal aristocracy, was a bustling city. Settled picturesquely on a tight peninsula between the Ashley and Cooper Rivers, yet poised to receive steamers off the Atlantic, it was surely the capital of the south. At least the commerce capital. Its docks were crowded with schooners seven days a week and seaman were either loading or unloading goods and wares to and from France, the Orient, the Bahamas or from the eastern United States. Frequent exports to other lands included precious cloths, tobacco, gunpowder, cotton and molasses. The best the South had to offer the world. Streets were narrow, and although most were dirt, a few were dressed out in carefully laid brick or ballast stone, accented with masonry sidewalks. These were mostly found in heavier areas of commerce and in front of the more affluent homes.

Hoop-skirted women, refined and cultured, proud and haughty, sashayed along the streets like belles going to a ball, whether they were haggling in the marketplace or gossiping among themselves in a city park. The tongues were sharp, but the cold condescending stares at people less fortunate or lower in class were even more cutting.

As the Fishers locked arms and strolled at midday through the Charleston marketplace, they attracted the scornful eyes of passing women. Lavinia had no use for these pretentious, genteel socialites. When she intercepted their stares and whispers, she often let loose her tongue with words that might be heard only in the most vile of seaman's lairs. The women would then gasp and hustle off, wagging their own tongues, proclaiming their disgust. John would just smile that rakish smile, amazed at how those same callused lips that spat venomous obscenities could later be so passionately tender to his taste.

Lavinia was indeed beautiful. If not the most beautiful in the Carolinas, then certainly in Charleston. Like winter moonlight, bold, stunning, yet distant and cold. The lustful eye of a woman's husband would surely single her out as though all the other women on the street were suddenly invisible. A woman did not have to know her or know *of* her to detest her. Beauty begets envy, even jealousy. Lavinia had neither their education nor breeding, but that did not matter to the men. The stately gait, the perfect cheeks and the luscious, pink lips paralyzed rakes, rogues and the righteous alike. And then there were the eyes. Chameleon eyes that changed with mood. The fiery, steel blue eyes that when angry would thrust into the heart like the point of a rapier. Or the icy, contemptuous eyes that reflected apathy and disgust for the affluent and the corpulent. And the soft, alluring summer eyes. Eyes that could summon the loins of any man. Bedroom eyes that made love with every slow, calculating closing of their lids. Whatever their look, men were either disarmed by them or were compelled to look away in fear for their souls.

As he was forced to behave this day like any other day when he accompanied Lavinia, John still showed his disdain through gritted teeth when the lechers in their fine wear undressed her with their eyes. Although his temper flared when his own eyes met the men's leers, had he ever acted on his jealousy by raising a fist against another, most of the men, whether gentlemen or ruffians, could have bested him, and he would be humiliated in front of his wife.

Today her long raven hair was pinned up tightly by the two tortoise-shell combs that had been sent to her anonymously. She knew they were from Matthew, as they appeared in a package left on their veranda only days after the parson had returned from the voyage to Ireland where he buried his mother. The pin-up style allowed her to appear more sophisticated and refined than she actually was. If she had only been born of bluer blood and could learn to stifle her cobra tongue, she could very well have been the Queen of the Charleston socialites.

The faces of aristocracy in Charleston were pale, depicting the affluent women's wealth and status. Only a field woman's face would be burned or tanned from the sun. That was the first telltale of one's status. Although Lavinia left the farming and tending of livestock to John, she neither avoided the sun nor protected her face with a bonnet. She often allowed her face to drink in the sun as though it were warm nectar. The sun was life and she sometimes found herself dancing in its rays. The sun made her happy, just as gray days brought on gloom. It was her tanned, radiant face that told the Charleston society that she was little more than slave class. Their accusatory, punishing eyes did not faze her, however, for she flaunted her beauty in their faces, intimidating them with her full, ripe bosom that accentuated her small waist, a waist never strangled by a corset. And her eyes could retaliate against the most contemptuous glares as she could fire icy barbs at the women without saying a word. Yet, she could turn her eyes onto the woman's husband and seduce him with a sultry, hypnotic stare.

Every handsome, ebullient young man under thirty-five caught her attention. She was given to such flirtatious, histrionic behaviors when John was not around, compelling men to follow her as though she were a Pied Piper. They caught the scent of her lilac water, and coupled with her sensuous smile and seductive presence, she could easily have ensnared the lot. As she allowed the dashing rakes to make over her, other men were the objects of her scorn. Lavinia despised the police, all politicians and judges, and abhorred fat, balding and elderly men. She made no bones about her disdain for them.

Although she was little more than a tease, she never strayed from her vows. Whatever she was, and whatever love she kept in her bosom for Matthew, she was no adulteress. She loved John too much to behave like a whore.

There had been only four people at their wedding: Lavinia and John, the Justice of the Peace, and his wife. However, one would think the two of them were married before the congregation at St. Michael's. As Lavinia's wedding was the most special moment of her life, she had paid over twenty dollars for the white Versailles gown she had shipped to her from Paris through Longworth's of Charleston. Her mother's cameo broach adorned the lace neckpiece that lay against her silken throat. The antique pendant first belonged to her grandmother in 1756 and had accessorized all three of the women's dresses at their weddings. She often took the gown from her closet to model it in front of the mirror. John was amused, watching her, but she needed to see herself in it a dozen times a year, especially on those days she was down, to re-enact that happy day of her wedding. It still fit her as sweetly as it did nine years before. It was the day John had rescued her from a life of loneliness, a solace that she herself had created by snuffing out the life of her aunt.

The old woman was conniving and greedy. She had her sights set on the sole ownership of Six Mile House and Lavinia could never allow that to happen. Aunt Fiona, despite her religious fanaticism, had a lust for money and material things. She had squandered what little cash Lavinia's parents had in the bank on worthless trinkets, ugly dresses and dark, gaudy drapes. As the woman always said that she was anxious to meet Jesus one day, Lavinia saw to it that her quest was hastened and cheerfully set up the meeting. She mixed the sleeping powder into the woman's nightly cup of tea and once Aunt Fiona was catatonic in her rocker, Lavinia took a goose down pillow and buried it in the woman's face until her breathing stopped. There was no reason to suspect the pretty eighteen year-old of murder, especially when she told the authorities of her aunt's sickly days. The tears had spilled like raindrops from her lovely, convincing eyes, and neither the physician nor mortician chose to examine the corpse for foul play. They assumed the ill, fifty-five year-old woman died of natural causes.

Aunt Fiona was interred beside her sister, Lavinia's mother. The night she was buried, a sneering Lavinia strolled contemptuously to the gravesite and with cup in hand, poured the steaming liquid onto the freshly-turned soil, saying "Your evening tea, auntie dear."

John left Lavinia at the bank on Holt Street to meet with his friend Joe Roberts at a tavern for a tankard of ale. "Do not tarry, John Fisher," she chided. "It will take me only a matter of minutes to pick up the fabric your weak mind forgot, yesterday. I will also not have you in any drunken state this day, so limit your ale. If you do not heed what I say, then you will find your way back to Six Mile on your own."

"Yes, my princess." He removed his hat and bowed sarcastically. Lavinia jabbed him in the ribs with her parasol. He laughed, then turned on heel toward the pub.

"At the buggy," she called after him. "Be at the buggy in one hour!"

He threw up a hand to acknowledge the order without looking back.

As Lavinia whisked along the streets on her way to the fabric store, her dark rose dress made a swishing noise against her petticoat. She looked provocatively in the direction of handsome young men, whose eyes willingly reciprocated. Beneath their tailored coats, she took account of the broad chests that filled out stylish vests and shirts. The tight trousers and leggings revealed masculine thigh and calf muscles. Some of these dandies were in the company of their wives; but that did not matter to Lavinia. She loved making the women seethe nearly as much as she enjoyed turning their husbands' heads. They squinted their eyes contemptuously, all the while clutching their husbands' arms, else they be snatched away by the notorious Lavinia Fisher. Each gentleman touched the brim of his hat, meeting Lavinia's seductive blue eyes with theirs, then dropped them down a bit to appreciate her abundant, ripe bosom. All this street drama not only empowered Lavinia but gave her a sense of presence and notoriety, even if it was one of community disdain

"There she is, the whore of Six Mile House," the woman whispered loudly to her friend as they passed Lavinia.

"My pardon, madam. Did you say something about me?"

Lavinia's retort startled the women. They stopped, but kept their distance. Either they didn't expect Lavinia to hear the remark or it was intended to be loud enough to provoke or ridicule her. The woman who made the comment, a large-set, matronly crone in a plain black dress with matching bonnet, tightened the muscles in her face and stared arrogantly into Lavinia's eyes. "Only that a woman on the street dressed as you are with bosom exposed conjures up ideas of whoredom, and if you must know, many of the decent women of Charleston have you on their tongues. Do everyone a favor and refrain from making these embarrassing appearances on our streets."

Lavinia moved to within three feet of the woman. Bearing down on her with her own imperious eyes, she replied "Madam, as your gossip pours over this town like bootleg liquor spilling into the crevices of Charleston's ballast stone, I will give you something to talk about. But you must first keep your husband away from my bed. I do hope he is more of a man between your legs than he is between mine."

Uproarious laughter was heard in the vicinity of a bench by the mercantile. Two elderly men, who could not help but eavesdrop on the conversation, slapped their knees in amusement while making inarticulate noises of merriment. The guffaws enraged the two socialites.

"You are an insolent and despicable girl. How dare you shame me to my friend and these men!" the woman retorted.

"You shame yourself, madam," Lavinia responded. "By lying as a cold, dead carp under your sheets, compelling your poor husband to fish other ponds."

More laughter erupted from the men, which this time sent the woman and her friend off in a wordless huff. One of the men called out to Lavinia. "My word, girl. You don't make many friends in this town, do you?" He laughed again and although the men had served her as pawns, she found the men to be equally disgusting.

Lavinia normally enjoyed the streets of Charleston, especially on spring or summer evenings. The golden flicker of gas lamps on shop walls and street corners signaled the end of the day's commerce and the coming dusk. Fancy women may be seen stepping into fine coaches that would carry them to their stately Greek Revival homes. Some boasted an air of haughtiness and self-importance, while others appeared genuine and unpretentious. A part of Lavinia wondered what it would be like to taste just a small morsel of the city's social flavor. Occasionally she might catch a glimpse of a kind of soiree in one of the houses on Queen or Beaufain Street. Sometimes stopping to peer into a window, she took in the carefully coifed women in colorful gowns gliding across the floor of a grand parlor in the arms of handsome and grotesque men alike in step with a Mozart waltz. The rooms decorated with lavish wallpaper may have twelve-foot ceilings from which hung magnificently ornate chandeliers. She stood like a street waif whose face reflected the yellow glow of the lighted room that from one's vantage from the inside made her appear ghostly. Her world ran paradoxical to theirs. Her world was where liquor ran freely, where cards lay on the table and where the odor of tobacco tainted the purity of the room.

There was a part of her that rejected and deprecated such goings on as these ostentatious social gatherings. It did not matter to her whether anyone liked her; it saved her the trouble of liking them back. She didn't need or want to be anything like these phony women. After all, in the conduct of her business, she was more powerful than the lot.

Chauncey Harriman sat at his desk picking his teeth and mulling over some legal documents in advance of a runaway slave's trial. There was no doubt the man would be hanged, but as there had been incidents of political activism and growing abolitionist sympathizing among the constituents, he would be compelled to give even a being he valued as "one species above a mule" a fair trial. Or at least go through the motions. His recent admonishment of the *Charleston Free Press* and the altercation with Cleary had not won him many friends. In fact, there was a virulent hatred for him by most. But he was a powerful man and an accumulation of friends was not paramount to him. It did not matter to him that women reported to their husbands that he had touched them or frotteured against their buttocks in social gatherings.

Harriman was also known to be uncommonly cruel to his slave family. Although he did not whip the slave woman who tended his ill wife and prepared his meals, her husband, Marcus, a tall, strapping man in his upper thirties, did bear the scars from his whip for even the most trivial of sins. On one occasion, Marcus allowed the horse to bolt, causing the buggy to jolt forward, snapping back Harriman's neck. There was yet another, more felonious offense where Marcus burned a hole in Harriman's Persian rug while lighting his master's pipe. For these two grave transgressions alone, Harriman laid open his slave's back until the blood ran, then oozed for days from the massive skin tears. The magistrate boasted that he had hung more than thirty runaway slaves in his tenure and informed Marcus that if he continued in his erring ways, he would put the rope on the man's neck himself and leave him for the crows.

Suspected pirates and thieves were likewise swiftly tried on largely unsubstantiated evidence. He would say the men must be guilty, because they could not look him in the eye. Harriman charged the jury to perform its rightful duty and not disgrace the judicial system. This meant bringing back a guilty verdict, or else face the wrath of the man known as Hanging Harry.

Clearing the last step to Meeting Street from the courthouse, the fat man, followed by his servant, Marcus, caught sight of Lavinia as she approached his direction. In passing, Chauncey Harriman pretended to be paying no attention to human traffic while rebuking Marcus about something, then by accident, bumped into her. When her hundred fifteen pound frame collided with the tub of lard nearly twice her weight, she lost her balance. This gave Chauncey the opportunity to thrust his large hands onto her shoulders to steady her.

"Why, Lavinia. I do apologize for my clumsiness. I did not see you." He flashed an evil grin that revealed a mouthful of very bad teeth.

She knew this was a lie because she had intercepted his leer while he was still descending the courthouse steps.

"I am sorry, sir, but how do you know my name?"

"It is my business to know everyone in this town, especially citizens as lovely as you. I am Justice Chauncey Harriman, the city's magistrate." His bulging eyes and ruddy, pig-like face repulsed her. He was physically imposing at better than six feet with thick meaty hands and bulging waist. The dingy powdered wig lay crooked on his fat head and gravy stains from the day's lunch were caked in the corners of his mouth. Lavinia nearly gagged at the smell of his foul breath.

"You are the mistress of the inn to the north of here, if I am correct," he said.

"You are, sir. The inn has been my home for more than twenty-eight years."

The magistrate stood for a moment making love to her body with his eyes, not speaking further. His lechery nauseated her and she was tempted to pull the stiletto from her sleeve and slide it slowly, but forcefully, into his corpulent stomach. She tried in vain to stifle her half-smile, imaging that he would surely pop like some gigantic blood tick.

Harriman mistook the smile as a sign of interest. "Perhaps the lady would care to join me for a glass of port at McCrady's Longroom?"

"I think not, sir. I must meet my husband within the hour." Lavinia backed away to gather distance from the man.

"Well, one day I shall visit your inn to dine or take a sabbatical from my horrid wife and spend the night." He grinned, displaying his bilious yellow teeth, then flicked his tongue over the gravy stains like a lizard.

"It would be an honor, sir" she lied. "And I would be most pleased to have you sample my special blend of tea before you retire." She smiled again. This time it was a wicked smile.

As Lavinia strode away in brisk determination, Harriman's blood flushed and raced to his loins at the thought of bedding down the fiery vixen. He would indeed have his way with her, husband or not. He heard John Fisher was a mouse, an insignificant speck of scrapple, whom Harriman would gleefully let watch while he lifted the skirt of the juicy Lavinia to split her in two with his noble staff. He licked his bulbous lips yet again.

CHAPTER FOUR

Two mornings later a crusty wagoner crossed the intersection on Old Dorchester at Callie's Landing finding that a small tree had fallen across the full width of the lane. As he pulled his team to a halt, a lone masked rider approached from his right and pointed his flintlock within three feet of the old man's head. The driver quickly dropped the reins and lifted his hands. Three other riders, also each wearing hats pulled down over full-face cloth masks and toting rifles, surrounded his wagon.

"What's in the crates?" barked one of the highwaymen.

"Rice. Just rice, that's all. What would you ever want with it?"

"Didn't say we wanted anything with it. But that ain't what you're haulin'. Pull back that tarp and let's see what else you got."

The man stroked his white beard and hesitated a moment before replying. "Ain't nothin' under there 'cept my travel bag with a bunch of clothes in it. You fellers interested in my underwear, are ye?"

"Don't be impudent, old man. Just dig it out and toss it on the ground," demanded the rider to his left.

The driver edged his fingers ever so slowly along his thigh and touched the barrel of his rifle lying against the seat bottom.

"Eh eh!" chided the same bandit. "Kick it off the wagon. You don't want to die today."

The man did so, vehemently displaying his hostility. He turned his head and shot a stream of tobacco juice into the breeze, partially collecting the cloak of one of the bandits. The old man then wiped his beard with his sleeve.

The bandit spoke again. "Now pull back the tarp!"

The wagoneer made it known he was not in any hurry, chomping like a cow chewing its cud on the wad of tobacco and eyeing each one of the bandits curiously. He especially studied a smallish rider set atop a beautiful roan, perhaps sixteen hands high. Obviously, he thought, she was a woman. The waist was small. The dark hair was pulled up tightly under a floppy brown hat and the legs were short and shapely under the tan riding pants.

"You're a woman, ain't cha?" The wagoner grinned beneath the scraggly, stained beard, baring his yellowed teeth.

The bandit edged his horse closer to the wagon and thrust his rifle under the man's nose. "You never mind about that, mister. Now I will tell you one more time. Drop that bag down!"

The driver appeared defiant with his continued slow movements, remaining interested in what he perceived to be the woman. "I know you, lady. You're the pretty thing from that inn up further on the road. Yessiree, I'd know that figure…."

Before the man could complete the last sentence of his life, the muzzle of the woman's rifle exploded with fire and smoke. The bullet smashed into the man's jaw, tearing away flesh and teeth and splattering a stream of blood and tobacco juice onto the mask of another bandit. The wagoner keeled off his seat and tumbled toward the front and onto the ground like a two hundred-pound sack of potatoes. The sharp report of the rifle caused the horses to bolt and the right front wheel ran over the man's head.

"Gawd!" the bandit on the right exclaimed. "You were pretty quick with the trigger, weren't you?"

"Would you have preferred he spill his guts to the police or spill his blood on this good Carolina soil? He said he recognized me. I had no choice."

The masks came off and the man named Roberts who had positioned his horse to the rear of the wagon broke open one of the crates with the butt of his rifle. "Aha! The old bastard lied, all right. He's a rum runner."

Indeed, each crate contained approximately thirty ruby-colored bottles of Puerto Rican rum that were likely smuggled into the Port of Charleston, bound for points north. And the old man's bag? It did contain a couple pairs of trousers, a flannel shirt and some very pitiful looking underwear.

"A fine booty today. What we don't keep for ourselves will bring a fine price from the taverns up the pike," said Fisher.

Roberts opened one of the bottles, took a swig and passed it on to Fisher, who then tossed it to Heyward. Lavinia then commanded, "Mr. Roberts, get the wagon off the road and hide it down in the barn at Five Mile House. John, dig a hole and plant the man's carcass, then get back to the house. I've got a hen sitting out for supper."

That was her way. It was all just business, the taking of life and property. But there was the business of the inn as well, and a guest could come along at any time.

On the 8th of November, a letter of inquiry was received in the office of the Honorable Chauncey Harriman, Chief Magistrate.

"My Dear Mr. Harriman:

This office has been approached by one Madeline Hastings, wife of William, whose husband was to effect business dealings with Farthmore Carriage Works and Sir Henry Middleton on or about the sixteenth of October. Said Mr. Hastings has not returned to his family nor has his wife received his letter explaining his whereabouts.

Would you be so kind as to inquire with the proprietor of the carriage house and Master Middleton if they have met with Mr. Hastings?

Mrs. Hastings avows there remains no discord between them and it is unlike Mr. Hastings to have spent more than three days in his travels from home without penning a letter to his wife.

I respectfully await your word regarding this imperative matter. I remain your humble servant,

Samuel Johannson
Attorney at Law
Philadelphia"

Upon reading the letter, Harriman sucked a particle of chicken from between his front teeth and tossed the letter toward his servant, Marcus. "Boy, take this to Sheriff Cleary and be quick about it." Marcus shuffled into the room with head down and picked it up from the floor. "Get on with you before you taste the sting of my whip!" said Harriman.

Marcus shot him a quick glance of contempt, then dropped his eyes quickly, bowing before leaving the magistrate's office.

"Worthless, he is", muttered Harriman. "If he moves any slower, the sun will set before he manages two blocks."

Marcus stood about six feet one with charcoal-black skin and prominent veins that accentuated the strength in his muscular forearms and hands. Strong weathered hands that depicted a hard-labor history. He had taken the surname of Washington after the great President had died twenty years before. Until then, he had only been known as Marcus, first the property of Daniel Jarvis, then Harriman. He had been a man with no identity except *slave*. But his children needed names like other humans and the name felt good to him. Harriman did not recognize Marcus' surname, as it was disrespectful and even criminal for a sub-human to have the last name of the Father of the Country.

At home in the brick one room, dirt floor quarters that had been a carriage house, Marcus, his wife, and two teenage sons lived behind the white-washed three-story known as Harriman House. His master often hired out the two boys to the wealthy Robert Tillman to tend his horses and mules, clean the stables and work the rice and tobacco fields on the Tillman Plantation. Marcus was pleased with this arrangement for he knew if his sons slaved in some capacity for Harriman, he would find fault with their toil and they too would be cut to ribbons by the ruthless monger.

"Chief Cleary, suh." Marcus called out from the doorway, slightly humped and sulking, making no eye contact. His voice resonated in a rich baritone.

"Yes, Marcus. What is it?"

"Massa Chauncey. He say to give dis to you."

Cleary beckoned him forward, then held out his hand to take the paper. "Thank you, Marcus." He laid the envelope on his desk and leaned on his elbows. "How are Kendra and your boys?"

Marcus appeared dazed, not fully digesting Cleary's interest in his family or his kind demeanor. "Fine, suh. Jus' fine." The eyes were not so oppressed and intimidated now.

Cleary then opened the envelope, took out the letter, then looked up at Marcus. "Did the magistrate give you any instructions with this?"

"Naw suh. Jus' said to bring it."

"Okay," replied the chief, rising from his desk. "Tell the man I will look at it, then get back to him." Marcus bowed, then returned to his skulking position and slowly exited the room.

"Wait, Marcus. Take this basket of apples to your family. The widow Dickenson brought these to me this morning. I've told her a dozen times that apples do not agree with my digestion. Maybe that's why she keeps bringing them to me. She has some kind of desire to kill me." Cleary smiled wryly, giving the apples a wince.

This prompted a smile from Marcus, a facial expression Cleary had never seen on the man. It was as though the sun had finally come out onto a mountain eroded by years of hard winter and gloom. "Thank you, suh. My wife will prolly make 'em into one of her pies."

Cleary nodded. "Yes, and I have a feeling the pie will end up in the magistrate's big gut."

Marcus' smile broke out into a grin, but then it went away just as quickly as it appeared. He knew Cleary was right. If Harriman caught a whiff of the aroma, he would likely consume the whole pie. The face of the slave man was cold and troubled again, as he would return to the courthouse and the atmosphere of ridicule and degradation. Marcus bowed again, making Cleary uncomfortable, and shut the door behind him.

The Chief Constable read the letter then called in Constable Miller to ready his carriage. A half hour later, the two policemen arrived at Farthmore's shop on Trade Street. One of the coach builders standing outside the door of the business and capturing a smoke, dipped his head in respect to Cleary. Motioning to the man, Cleary said "Sir, would you kindly get Mr. Farthmore for me?" The man tossed his cigarette into a nearby drain and nodded, retreating into the building.

In a moment, a distinguished-looking, well-dressed gentleman in a white wig bearing the fine appearance of a snowy egret opened the door and approached the carriage. Cleary stepped down, extending his hand. "Master Farthmore, do I find you well today?"

"Good day, Chief Constable. Yes, indeed. I believe I am finally getting over my painful attack of the gout. This is the first day in a week I have been able to get my left shoe on."

"You must refrain from the rich meats and port, my friend, else you will have more and frequent episodes," Cleary chided. He then paused and took from his coat pocket the letter. "I am here on a matter of some concern. I hold here a letter from a Philadelphia lawyer, inquiring as to whether one Mr. William Hastings ever arrived in Charleston to conduct business with you. Have you seen such a man?"

"No. And it has infuriated me these weeks that he did not honor his contract with me on the Stafford we built for him. Now I am out this labor and money unless I am able to sell it to another. And that is improbable, for my sales have been thin and there is no market for another livery coach in this town. At least that I know of."

Cleary pursed his lips and nodded. "I see. Well, if he does appear, I ask that you instruct the man to see me, immediately." The chief then turned to Miller and said "Malcolm, please take the carriage to Governor Middleton's place and make the same inquiry. I hold no hope that he went there, having not been here first. Master Farthmore, will you be so kind as to deliver me back to the jail?"

"I will, sir." Then he stopped and put a thoughtful finger to his lips. "Let me get for you Hastings' letter and contract. Perhaps you will be able to extract a clue from these documents." The two men went into the office and after fumbling through the secretary cluttered with a myriad of papers, Farthmore retrieved Hastings' letter and promissory note. "Here, you may look these over."

The letter spelled out the specifications of the features and accessories to be built into the Stafford as well as Hastings' tentative arrival date. He was to stop along the way in Florence just south of the North Carolina border to visit a cousin, James Connolly, a sort of hero who had ridden with Frances Marion, the

Swamp Fox, having captured a British general who was found lying with a Carolina concubine in her house along the Pee Dee.

"I will send Master Connolly a letter to learn if Hastings did indeed stop at his place. There is little more I can do, except make further inquiries about the city."

CHAPTER FIVE

On November 20th, Cleary received a return letter from Connolly affirming that Hastings had stayed the night with him on the 14th of October, then set out about four the next morning for Charleston with the full moon at his back. Cleary surmised that Hastings' route from Florence had to bring him along the Goose Creek Road just north of Charleston; however, something could have happened to the lone rider anywhere along his journey through South Carolina. He could have been set upon by robbers, especially the band of outlaws called the Swamp Rats, known for their vicious work along the Black River. Remnant braves of the Creek Nation had also terrorized settlers and journeymen alike for over a century. If Hastings had made it to Charleston, Cleary estimated that with a combination of gallop and walk along the hundred-mile stretch, he should have put himself in the city by the late afternoon or evening of the 15th.

As expected, Cleary's man had learned from Middleton that Hastings did not materialize on his estate. The mount promised to the Philadelphian was sold to another.

The magistrate, Harriman, in his usual callused manner, sent Colonel Cleary a scathing message demanding to know why Hastings had not been located and why the Chief Constable had neglected to conduct a thorough investigation. The tone of the letter and the insinuation of police incompetence summoned Cleary's anger; but discretion being the better part of valor, he decided no reply was better than yet another confrontation. However, he did instruct Miller on the morning of 22nd to prepare his carriage and to accompany him for a canvass of the populace up to twenty miles north of the city and to the limit of his jurisdiction.

The constables began their inquiries just south of Goose Creek along the Ashley, stopping at inns, blacksmith shops, taverns and houses to ask the people of the area whether they remembered a man named William Hastings. As Cleary had no description of the man, he could only ask them about a lone traveler who may have stopped at their establishments for a lunch or ale in the middle of October. As strangers had patronized their businesses on a daily basis, it was difficult for anyone to single out any one individual; and furthermore, names were rarely exchanged.

It was nearly three-thirty when Cleary and Miller, combing their way back south along the Old Dorchester Road, arrived at Six Mile House. As Miller pulled in the reins near the gateposts, they spied John Fisher cutting brush with a scythe on the upper field behind the house. Lavinia, hearing their approach, opened the front door and stepped onto the porch.

"Good day, Madam," called Cleary. "Are you the inn's proprietress?"

"My husband and I own the inn, yes. Are you gentlemen looking for lodging this evening?"

"No," replied Cleary, removing his hat. "I am Chief Constable Colonel Nathaniel Cleary from Charleston. This is my lieutenant, Malcolm Miller. May we have a word?"

"You may, sir. Please come in. My name is Lavinia Fisher and my husband, John, is in the back. Would you like a cold drink, as you look well-traveled and parched?"

Miller spoke up, hat in hand, eyeing the woman's beauty. "Thank you, ma'am, we would indeed." With his mouth open and eyes fixed in awe, he appeared as eager as a beagle to be in Lavinia's company. The two men dismounted the buggy and proceeded toward the porch.

"I have cool water, fresh cider or I could draw you some ale."

"The water will be just fine for us," said Cleary, giving Miller a quick glance, knowing he would prefer the stronger drink. "We are on official business and cannot stay long."

Lavinia motioned for the men to each take a rocker then went into the house to prepare their drink. After downing the first glass in scarcely four gulps and touching his dripping mouth to his shirtsleeve, Miller handed the tumbler back to Lavinia for a refill. Cleary, who was still sipping his water politely, raised his eyebrows and drew one corner of his mouth into a smile at his officer's unrefined behavior.

"My lady, have I not seen you about town on occasion?" asked the chief.

"Perhaps, sir. Although the business of the inn does not allow me to be as frequent in the city these days."

Cleary settled back a little in the rocker, appearing to be in some thought. Keeping his eyes steadfastly on Lavinia's and stroking his chin, he nodded slightly. "Lavinia. Tis a nice name." He then raised one finger, indicating a memory spark. "Now I remember. Some years ago, it was your parents who met ill fate here at the hands of the Indians. You were just a child then. I do regret that sorrowful incident. It appears you have done well for yourself here in spite of your terrible experience."

"I have managed, Mr. Cleary. My husband has helped me through many sad recollections. As it took me a while to regain my spirit, Mr. Fisher's love and support have sustained me."

"Fisher," uttered Miller. "I know some Fishers in the city."

"My husband would be no relation, Mr. Miller. He is from Savannah." Lavinia then turned her face toward Cleary. "I do know of you, sir, and your excellent reputation as a fair and noble policeman. I am most pleased to make your acquaintance."

"Likewise." Cleary stood, bowed slightly and clicked the heels of his boots. He then slowly dropped into the rocker, again.

"What business brings you by here, sir?" Lavinia tried not to show her uneasiness, suspecting the reason for their visit.

"A traveler named William Hastings has disappeared on his way here from Philadelphia. His family is most concerned that he has not returned home having been gone nearly six weeks. Have you seen the man, Mrs. Fisher?" asked Cleary.

"I am not sure, sir. What were his features?"

"That I cannot tell you as no one has provided a description. But I must ask you officially if a man named Hastings boarded here at any time?"

Lavinia swallowed hard, then with an unwavering, unflinching response, as true as she could make her answer sound without raising suspicion, she replied "No, sir. You are free to check my ledger or search the house. I have scarcely had three boarders since July, but none with the name of Hastings. My husband will verify this as well."

Cleary studied her a bit, but appeared satisfied with her answer. "That will not be necessary. I will ask you, however, that if the man does venture this way to please send word to me immediately."

"That I will, sir."

Cleary clicked his heels again, took the hand that she extended and in noble gesture, lightly kissed her fingers. Though her heart was still racing from Cleary's inquisition, she took note of how much a gentleman he was. Not stuffy or pompous as were most other aristocrats; rather he was refreshingly genuine. She noted as well his stately posture and handsome jaw. A good man, all right. Too bad he was on the wrong side of the law and may well become her enemy.

Cleary and Miller donned their hats again, then proceeded toward their carriage. When they settled in, Miller slapped the hindquarters of the horse with the reins and made a clicking sound with his mouth. After a mile or so to the south, Miller looked at Cleary and sighed. "That was indeed a beautiful woman, Chief Constable."

Cleary nodded. "Indeed, Malcolm." He then looked off to the side of the road in thoughtful pose. "But would not a 'no I have not seen the man' sufficed?"

"I do not follow you, sir."

"She invited us to check her ledger and affirm such with her husband. Does that not seem strange and overdone? She appeared defensive without having reason to be. Furthermore, I have heard the name Fisher associated with one of the bands of robbers operating in these parts."

"I have heard the same," said Miller. "I suppose I was so duped by her loveliness, a steed could have run me down and I wouldn't have been fazed."

"You are too much for the ladies, Miller. If you would focus more on your objectivity than a well-turned ankle, your insight would be keener." Cleary turned his head back to the constable and smiled.

"Yes, Chief Constable," Miller replied, somewhat embarrassed.

The men continued south along Old Dorchester to another inn and tavern, finding no luck. At dusk they entered the city via the Ashley Bridge, giving up their investigation for the day.

As soon as the constables had departed Six Mile House, John Fisher hurried down from the field to learn the identity of the men and nature of their business.

"They were policemen, John, inquiring about Hastings."

"Gawd, Lavinia. Do they suspect he was here?"

"Don't get your bowels in an uproar. They know nothing. They were well satisfied that we never saw the man. They appeared more interested in giving me the look-over. The smaller constable only sat there and grinned like a chessie cat when my eyes met his."

Fisher grimaced and stroked his broad mustache. "Don't always be so sure your looks will cast a spell on every man, Lavinia. There are shrewd men out there that will not always be so easily swayed."

Lavinia moved closely to him, sweeping his dark hair behind an ear with her fingers, then placing her lips within inches of his. She whispered "And are you one of those men, John Fisher?"

He leaned into her to kiss the lips, but she pulled her head back abruptly.

"Stronger, more determined men than you have not been able to resist me, my darling," she teased.

"My Dear Mrs. Hastings:

This office has been charged to investigate the disappearance of your husband, William, who was to effect business with Masters Farthmore and Middleton, the former Governor of our state. To this date, our efforts to locate him have proved futile. As we have made inquiries to all who could possibly have seen him, no person has admitted meeting him.

Our investigation will remain active as we continue to search for Mr. Hastings. I will ask that you provide to me a description of his physical characteristics, manner of clothing and type of horse. This information will greatly facilitate our investigation.

I have undertaken this matter personally, having realized your fears for his safe return. Please convey this letter to your attorney Mr. Johannson. I remain your humble servant,

Nathaniel Cleary
Chief of Police
City of Charleston
South Carolina"
November 24, 1818.

The year ended and there was no further word about William Hastings. Cleary received another letter after Christmas, this time from Mrs. Hastings. The tone was sorrowful as expected, but there was also an element of frustration that he had not been successful in locating her husband. Seeing the New Year in without Mr. Hastings would surely consume her and she did not know whether she would indeed survive.

John Fisher's friend, William Heyward, a ruffian from the Charleston dock and distant cousin of George Washington's friend, frequented Six Mile House two or three nights a week. He and John generally played poker and drank Scotch whiskey until Lavinia indicated she had had enough and put him out. As Heyward knew about the Fishers' other 'business' and even assisted in body disposal on occasion, Lavinia reluctantly condoned the man, mainly because of her husband's friendship with him. But he also knew too much and she was not sure he could be trusted, especially considering alcohol seemed to loosen his lips. As Heyward was a regular at Dugan's Tavern near the dock, Lavinia would not have been surprised if yesterday's visit by the constable were spurred by Heyward's drunken account of the Fishers' misdeeds in the presence of a comrade across a bar table. One day she would also have to dispose of Heyward, friend or not, as he was indeed a threat.

At about three o'clock on February 17th a knock at the front door stirred the two men from their game and Fisher rose from the table to respond. A man, perhaps thirty, and boasting a boyish, but handsome face, stood in the doorway with a small bag in his hand.

"Good afternoon, sir. Have you a room for the night?"

Fisher took an unlit cigar butt out of his mouth and eyed the stranger for a moment, then replied "Yes, of course, Mister..."

"Peeples, John Peeples."

From the gaming table Heyward's slurred voice shouted, "Is this the bloke that interrupted our game?"

Lavinia, who had entered the parlor from the stairs, walked to the drunken man and said in a stern voice, "Mr. Heyward, I will kindly ask you to lower your voice and be respectful to our guest." Her blue eyes drilled holes into his, and knowing Lavinia's wrath, he nodded and dropped his head.

She went to Peeples and performed a sensuous curtsy. "My apologies for our loud friend. It appears his liquor has consumed his manners. My name is Lavinia and the man who greeted you is my husband, John."

"Hello, Lavinia. My name is John as well." He extended his hand to her.

"Yes, I heard. Welcome, Mr. Peeples. Would you also like some dinner? Our fare is one dollar for lodging and another dollar for both dinner and breakfast."

"I sure would, ma'am. Would you point out my room? I need to wash some of this dust off my bones. I'll need a tub for bathing, if you have one."

Lavinia gestured toward the hallway and asked him to follow her. "I'll prepare you a bucket of hot water for your bath. Dinner will be at four-thirty today. I hope you like smokehouse ham and apple pie."

"I don't mind telling you I'm famished. Been on the road all day without as much as a morsel."

When Lavinia set the steaming bucket and fragrant soap in the bath room, she returned to the table where Heyward sat and squared off with him again. "Heyward, friend or not of John Fisher, if you ever conduct yourself as a drunken ass in the presence of a guest again, I will take my paring knife and carve up your genitals so that you are incapable of ever fathering children...that is, should your wife Elizabeth or any lowly whore ever wish to conceive with you."

Heyward looked in John's direction for help, but there was to be none. "She's right, you know. So keep a civil tongue this evening around Peeples or you'll neither stay for dinner nor share any profits that may find their way into our pockets."

"Hell, John. Do you really think the blaggart has anything? He looks like a commoner and I'll wager he has only enough money on him to pay his room and board."

"We'll see. If I know Lavinia, she'll get him to open up at the dinner table."

"Keep your voices down," Lavinia chided. "You know how they will carry down the hallway. And you, Heyward, keep your mouth closed at the table except when you're stuffing it with food."

Heyward set his glass of bourbon down and nodded. "I hear you, Laviny. I'll behave myself."

Promptly at four-thirty, Peeples left his room, made his way across the creaking hall floor and entered the dining room. Lavinia stood over the dining table, placing red cloth napkins into pewter rings and setting out her mother's Edenborough silverware. She was lovely to him with her hair pinned up, wearing a powder-blue dress with fine lace on boile cloth and leg-o-mutton sleeves. And she smelled delightful.

"Dinner is ready, Mr. Peeples. Would you care for a glass of port to begin your meal?"

"Yes. Fine," he replied, standing respectfully behind his chair, waiting for Lavinia to seat herself. Her husband and Heyward were already seated and tearing at the cake of bread.

"You are indeed a gentleman, Mr. Peeples," she said, giving her man a sour look. "Unlike some men who have forgotten their Southern graces." John stood up immediately, as if commanded, but Heyward continued with the tearing and buttering.

As the others began to eat, Peeples bowed his head to say a silent prayer over the meal, and Lavinia, seeing this, shot glares at her husband and Heyward for them to stop shoveling until the guest was finished. After his brief meditation, the men began again their frenzied attack on the food.

"From where do you hail, Mr. Peeples, and if I am not too personal, what business are you in?" asked the hostess.

He chewed what was in his mouth, holding up a finger until he swallowed, then responded. "I am from Georgia, near Albany. I do a little farming and trapping, mostly the trapping. I sold a few pelts on the way here and made quite more than I expected to get for the whole lot. The remainder of the pelts, I hope to unload on the furrier in Charleston tomorrow. I heard they bring the highest dollar there in two states."

Lavinia smiled at him, not pretentiously, but with genuineness. She actually thought him to be refreshing company, especially considering her ill-mannered husband and his obnoxious friend. "I trust you will do well with your furs tomorrow. However, for tonight, we shall be making you as comfortable as possible," she said.

As the conversation between Lavinia and Peeples contin-ued, he found himself taken with her charm and beauty. He readily saw that she was an enigma, as she exuded an enticing blend of sexuality, grace and even frailty, frail as fine parchment, yet capable of a bitchy tongue and venomous stare when it came to the two offensive dinner companions. He noticed that her eyes could be contemptuously piercing one moment and tempes-tuously sensual the next. She was every bit the seductress in the way she moved, spoke and made love with her eyes.

Although Peeples was comfortable with Lavinia, he was not so much at ease with Fisher and Heyward. They talked very little and if it were not their cold stares that unnerved him, it was their darting glances between them that summoned his mistrust. He thanked his warm hostess for her "most excellent meal" and she invited him to the veranda to enjoy the remainder of the unusually warm February evening.

After a while Lavinia came out to join him, bringing some lemon sugar cookies. As she set them down on a table by his chair, her arm accidentally brushed his face. She apologized, then put her hand softly onto his. Her touch and sweet smell stiffened his loins. A sense of guilt came over him at having such a response, when his trusting wife back in Albany lay missing him, lonely and apprehensive about his travels. But as Lavinia was close enough to his face that he could nearly taste her warm breath, he could not stop the blood rush. Her company was short-lived, however, as she returned to the kitchen.

Peeples breathed deeply to savor the last, lingering hint of her toilet water in his nostrils. From the east the rush of the wind off the Ashley compelled the branches of the oaks and pe-cans to begin their frantic talk, perhaps forewarning of a brew-ing storm. Most queer for February. The sky's color changed unsuspectingly, even magically, from blue to gold, then orange to gray, as the red ball slipped beyond the horizon. He lit a rolled cigarette and drew in the taste that reminded him of home. He missed his wife. Maybe the sweet Lavinia had made him miss her all the more. He then heard the vulgar laughter of the poker players in the room behind the walls and thought it violated the beautiful music of the coming night. It was now almost suddenly dark. The crickets and tree frogs began their symphony as a whippoorwill repeated its song over and over. Soon, in the black of night, it was as though the Carolina countryside had been seduced by the Prince of Darkness himself.

He sat on the veranda for nearly two hours, dichotomously listening to the sounds of nature and the annoying outbursts inside. It was near time to retire. At the moment he stood, Lavinia again appeared at the door and offered him a cup of spiced tea. She said it was always settling to her at bedtime. Took the edge off.

"Thank you, ma'am, but no. The properties in tea have always disagreed with me. I would never be able to sleep." He followed her to the parlor.

"How about a liquor or other drink?" she asked, blinking the seductive eyes.

"No Ma'am. I really can't have anything on my stomach this late. Thank you just the same."

Overhearing Lavinia's and Peeples' conversation, the two men at the gaming table ceased their own dialogue and looked at one another. Peeples was not making this easy. Would they have to resort to more violent means to end the man's life?

CHAPTER SIX

Peeples bid his hosts good evening and said he would look forward to that breakfast before leaving in the morning. As she heard the door to his room close, Lavinia was almost relieved. She rather liked John Peeples. He was polite and genuine, not to mention handsome. Not Matthew Cowher handsome, but good looking just the same. But he did remind her of Matthew in a way....a younger Matthew. Perhaps there was a way to steal his purse without taking his life in return. Anyway, she had not murdered *every* guest who boarded at Six Mile House.

After replacing his evening clothes with a night shirt, Peeples said a brief prayer for his wife and protection in his travels, then snuffed out the lantern with a quick burst of breath. The bed was comfortable, but the room was stuffy, so he leaned over and raised the window about ten inches. Lying back on his pillow, he took in a deep breath and sucked the fresh evening air into his nostrils. Sounds of the night spilled into the room. Black-billed rain crows sang their raspy arias announcing an approaching storm.

Both Heyward and Fisher were bent on killing Peeples and after they were sure he had turned in, they took two cigars from the jar and went outside to plot the matter. Off to the southwest flashes of distant lightning lit up the sky, highlighting the shadows of the conspirators. Fisher leaned against the fence rail less than twenty feet from the west side of the house by John Peeples' window. He struck a match off a post and lit both his and Heyward's cigars. Along with the breeze filtering in the window came the pungent smell of cigar smoke and the voices of the two men. It did not occur to Fisher that they were standing by the guest room window, or that the window was raised. The carry of their voices seemed to Peeples like the men were standing at the foot of his bed.

"Since the bastard wouldn't drink the poisoned tea, how're we gonna do this?" asked Heyward.

Peeples sat up in his bed and put his ear to the window. What were they talking about?

"Lavinia always took care of these matters and I've never had to physically kill a man. All I've ever done is dispose of the carcasses."

A shot of adrenaline tore through Peeples and his heart began to race. Were they talking about him? Were they plotting to kill *him*? He grabbed hold of the iron bedstead, noticing it was shaking in his hands.

"I guess we'll wait a while and be sure he's out. Then we'll put a bullet in his head," said Fisher, casually, as though he was talking about doing away with an old plug. "It's startin' to storm. Let's get to the porch."

"God!" Peeples said aloud in his head. Would he run now? No. They would see or hear him for sure. But if he didn't, he'd be dead by midnight. Why did they want to kill him? Surely the lovely Lavinia could not be in on this. But Fisher did say that she took care of these matters. Had she poisoned other guests as Fisher insinuated? The fact that his digestive system did not allow him to drink the tea actually saved his life. He had to do something quickly, for they would come for him soon.

Peeples could barely clothe himself as his hands were shaking like the palsy. He had to be quiet in putting on his boots to be sure one didn't tromp on the floor. Then how could he move across the floor, considering it creaked like the hallway? He took one easy step, felt the wood give and pop, waited a few seconds, then set the other foot down. Step by slow step he moved softly to the closet and opened the door. Thank God it did not creak. It was pitch black in the closet, but feeling around, he found two more pillows. Retracing himself back to the bed, he placed the pillows in a straight line with the third one, covering them all with the quilt. He could barely make out what it all looked like, but as the lightning illuminated the room with its split second flash, he did think the lump resembled a body sleeping undercover.

Rolling thunder followed the lightning now and Peeples figured it would do much to drown out any noise as he made his escape. He raised the window gently to its full open position and slowly put his head out in the direction of the porch. As the sky lit up once more he saw Fisher leaning over the banister on his elbows, sucking on the cigar. The end of the stogie appeared as a red coal. If he dropped from the window now, he would surely be seen.

A bolt hit just outside of the window and Peeples jumped back as though he had already been shot. He did figure the men wouldn't come for him while the storm raged; they would think the lightning and thunder kept him awake and then they would not have the element of surprise. As the wind began to gust, the blowing rain and erratic branches of the sycamore spanked the side of the house. The rain was now steady and hard, splashing onto the windowsill and bedcovers. But if they did come to kill him during the storm, he would have to hide.

His purse. He now remembered stupidly telling them he had made a lot of money already on his pelts. They wanted that money. He would leave the purse on the bed. Maybe they would just be satisfied with taking it and not put a bullet in the pillows. No. They were set on killing him. However, he would see to it they did not get his money. It was only about seventy dollars, but it would sustain his wife and him nearly all next year. He left the purse hanging on the bedstead with ten dollars in it. Perhaps finding something in it would not raise their suspicion. But when they disposed of the 'body', they would find he had indeed duped them and they would look for him. Peeples was now panicking. He did not know what to do now. If only he had a gun.

The rain stopped about as quickly as it began. The rumbling in the sky was fading and could now be heard beyond the Ashley. The lightning flickers in the eastern sky were dim and less frequent. Peeples sat huddled in the corner, waiting. Not for the killers, but for his brain to tell him to run or hide. Why couldn't he move? He heard the parlor clock strike eleven times. The raucous storm was now completely gone, making the silence of the night even more deafening. He thought he heard the hall floor creak. No. The men's voices were still audible on the porch. He waited. Another half-hour passed painfully slow.

A glossy flute of moonlight began to stream into the window, illuminating the bed, the dresser and the crumpled heap of a man huddling in a corner of the room. He could no longer hear the voices. Peeples stood and stepped as softly as he could two, three steps in the direction of the window. Suddenly, footsteps for sure in the hallway. The killers were outside the door. He had no opportunity to cross the room to the window without them hearing him. By the time he reached it, they would be on him. He ducked into the closet, dropped down and pulled the door within three or four inches of closing in order to see the intruders. It was scarcely a moment later when he heard them enter the room. There was just enough light from the moon rays for him to see the two skulking figures quietly negotiating the floorboards. One held a pointed object in his hand. Peeples knew it was a gun. His heart was throbbing out of his chest with every beat and the perspiration dripping from his forehead stung his eyes.

He thought it was Fisher who spied the purse hanging from the wrought-iron foot stead. The man then retrieved it and slung it around his neck. So it was Heyward who had the pistol. Peeples could make out his hulk of a shadow beside the smaller man with the purse. Fisher did not have the nerve to end Peeples' life. Heyward slowly raised the flintlock and pointed it at the pillows. The brilliant flash and deafening crack nearly stopped Peeples' heart for real. He became faint, but managed to hold on to the door facing to avoid spilling forward into the room. He must not pass out or his position would be given away and he would be dead for sure. The flash of the pistol had temporarily blinded the killers so they were not able to determine that the lumps on the bed were not John Peeples.

Fisher was also weak at the knees, as the event sickened him. He was still able to move, however, to the rear of the bed, pull down the wood lever at the base of the wall and flush what he believed to be Peeples' body into the cellar and onto the rotting body of William Hastings. The stench was more stagnant than putrid, thanks to the lye, but evident, nonetheless. Fisher promptly uprighted the bed, re-latching it to the flooring. Another smaller figure entered the room and Peeples heard Lavinia Fisher's voice. "So you did it after all. I thought we were letting this one go."

Peeples, though still in paralyzing fear, felt yet a new emotion. Immense sadness. This beautiful wisp of a woman, a killer, just like these other rattlesnakes.

She went to the desk, struck a match and lit the lantern. Looking at the bed, she exclaimed "The quilt. My mother's quilt! You dropped it with the body? How could you do that, John Fisher?"

Peeples now realized how much of a monster she really was. She was more concerned about the family quilt than the life of a human being. A chill entered his perspiring body and he was suddenly cold. He slowly pushed the closet door closed short of latching so the light from the lantern would not expose him.

Lavinia yanked the purse off her husband's neck and reached in to pull out the contents.

"Ten dollars! You are fools, both of you. You killed a man for mere pittance. My quilt was worth more to me than ten dollars!"

Fisher sat on the bed with his hands folded in his lap, sulking and drained. Lavinia's anger only added fuel to his nausea. He was used to a man passing on quietly from poisoned drink, but not from a sudden, direct kill. Now her shrieking voice...it was all too much for him.

"I'm going to bed, John," she said, hands on hips, eyes icy and contemptuous. "There will be no celebration between the sheets tonight. I am entirely put out with this matter and especially *you*. Your weakness disappoints me." She turned her back on the men and closed the door behind her.

"Goddamn it," Fisher said. "She'll be in a stew about this for days. Let's get the hell out of here." He blew out the lantern and the men left the room.

Peeples settled back in the floor of the closet and waited until he heard the hooves of Heyward's horse clear the yard and enter Old Dorchester. When there were no more creaks and squeaks from the Fishers' bedroom floor upstairs, Peeples pushed open the closet door, climbed quietly through the window and dropped to the ground. As he ran the hundred meters up the hill toward the barn, his breath escaped his chest. This compelled him to stop and double up to try getting it back. The hair on the back of his neck stood up as he imagined Fisher had somehow heard him and was close on foot behind. Turning to look again at the house, it was but a large ghostly wisp. The moon tried its best to penetrate the new fog that rose over the storm-haunted fields, allowing him to pick up any movement. To his relief, he saw none. After entering the barn, he struck a match to find his horse.

Finding the reins and bit hanging on a nail over his horse's head, he slipped them onto his horse and led the mare past the rail fence and into the far field. Having been disturbed, the Fishers' bull began to bellow. As Peeples feared this would summon the killers to their window, he jumped bareback onto his mount and galloped at a racer's clip toward the highway. Even if Fisher had heard him, he would never catch him.

Peeples did not slow his horse for nearly three miles along old Dorchester until the mare gave out. Realizing she could run no further, he jumped off and walked her the rest of the way. He still checked over his shoulder every few steps or stopped to listen for hoof beats behind him. The night was thick with deathly quiet. A cool breeze that had followed the storm tickled pine branches, spilling their pungent aroma into the night air. Tree frogs, who basked joyously in their wet surroundings on either side of the road, had stopped their chorus in mid-song upon his approach, as if their conductor had suddenly raised his wand. He quickened his pace, feeling a renewed sense of terror breathing down his neck. About one thirty in the morning he finally crossed the Ashley Bridge into Charleston. Now he had to find the authorities.

Peeples entered the city just before two, finding there was not a soul on the streets. He thought there should at least have been a roving policeman on his rounds. Riding down toward the shipping dock, he came upon an apparent vagrant sitting on a bench, turning up a bottle and sucking down the last few drops of bourbon.

"You there" Peeples called out. "Can you tell me where the city jail is? I need to find a constable."

The drunk, appearing alarmed and defensive, replied "I ain't done nothin', sir. Just a little drinkin', that's all. Don't take me to that pig sty."

"I'm not the police, mister. I just want to know how to get to the jail."

The man swayed back and forth in his intoxication, and mumbling something incoherent, laid his body down on the bench without another word.

Peeples was drained, physically and emotionally. Turning his horse around, he decided to give it up and find a safe place to sleep. In the bright moonlight he spied the stately spire of St. Michael's, looming above the trees like a beacon. After securing his horse to the hitch rail at side of the church, Peeples turned the knob to the front door. It was open. He had found sanctuary at last on this horrible night. The church smelled musty, but it smelled like peace. For the first time in hours his heart was not racing. He leaned over and kissed the pages of a large open Bible lying on a table in the rear of the large sanctuary, then prayed a short prayer of thanks for his divine deliverance.

Upon finding a seat in the last pew, he sat for nearly an hour, revisiting his night of terror. He still found it incredulous this had happened to him. When he closed his eyes, he saw both the sweet face of Lavinia Fisher, doting over him on the veranda at Six Mile House, and the devil's face through the partially opened closet door, licking her wicked lips while groping through his purse in search for money. Peeples cupped his brow with both hands. He was too tired to think about it anymore. As the pews were lined with small velvet cushions, he lay his head down on one. Sleep finally came over him.

CHAPTER SEVEN

When morning broke, she was still asleep. John was sitting up in a chair by the bed, where he had been most of the night, stewing. Things didn't go well at all with Peeples. Lavinia was right. They should have let the man be. He obviously was a poor man, making just enough to make ends meet; but why did he tell them he had made money on his furs on the way in from Georgia? It didn't make sense. John sat with his arms folded, staring at Lavinia's petite, comely body. What mood would she be in today? For now she was angelic. He loved watching her sleep. She breathed deeply and restfully, making small wiffly noises as she exhaled. The lovely eyes were closed, but fluttering. Perhaps she was dreaming of some exotic land beyond the great waters of the Atlantic where she and John lay on sugar-white sand under blue, blue skies.

Lavinia awoke, slowly, blinking in the bright sunshine that streamed through the distorted window glass. A tiny moth flitted against the pane, casting its dancing shadow inside the reflected square of light on the plank floor. She saw John watching her, but said not a word, turning her head away from him. Lavinia was not over the events of last night. She slid off the bed and went to the basin that lay on the drawer chest, cupped her hands, and gently applied the water to her face. She stood for a while, allowing the cool water to freshen her skin, then sat on the velvet cushion of the dresser chair in front of the mirror, brushing the thick, silken hair, black as a raven's coat. Today the azure blue eyes were cold and passionless, transfixed on the stranger that stared back at her through the glass. As premonitions had often invaded her dreams and then just as often, coming to pass, she had an uneasy feeling about this day. Fear came over her for perhaps the second time in her life. It was not the same kind of fear she felt the day she witnessed the slaughter of her family, but fear, just the same.

As per her daily ritual, around eight-thirty, Lavinia took a cup of robust coffee onto the veranda to sit in her mother's rocker and listen to the music of the morning. The air was cold and fresh, prompting her to pull the woolen shawl tightly around her shoulders. Wrens that had chattered noisily on a tree branch hanging within a foot of the porch took sudden flight upon her approach. A startled shiny-backed lizard scampered off into a crack in the floorboards at the speed of spilled mercury. Today the sunlight brought her only gloom and apprehension. Disappointments such as she experienced the night before always affected her mood, and since she was only ten dollars richer this morning in exchange for the life of the likeable John Peeples, it made her all the more melancholy. Off to the right of the house under a moss-adorned oak stood the gravestones of her family. She stared at them for a few moments with loving, sad eyes, then settled back in the chair to gaze into the looking glass of her memory.

"Mama!" called the child. "Look!" She pointed out to her mother the four savages riding upon the grounds.

The woman ceased cranking the handle on the pump and ran to her children. "Winslow! Quick! Take Lavinia up to the barn and hide!" She then called to her husband in the meadow. " James! Indians! Get the musket, quick!"

The father ran from the field toward the house, but one of the renegades intercepted him, brushing him with his pony and knocking him down. As he sprang to his feet in an attempt to pull the rider off his mount, an arrow shot through his neck with a sickening thud. It had undoubtedly severed his carotid artery as blood gushed from the side of his neck and down his arm. His wife pulled an axe off the chopping block and began flailing it in the direction of the renegade bowman. Dropping quickly off his horse the savage ducked one of her swings, then sliced her throat, severing flesh and muscle into the neck verte-brae. A harmony of whoops chilled the air as her head fell onto her husband's body. The children ran toward the barn, looking back over their shoulders in horror.

Winslow buried his little sister deep into the straw, then vainly tried to cover himself just as one of the cutthroats who had entered the doorway spotted him. When the boy attempted to climb the makeshift ladder into the loft, the renegade pulled him off and tossed him to the floor. Winslow retreated on his hands and buttocks, but the killer picked up a pitchfork by the door and without mercy, thrust it into the boy's abdomen. The man then withdrew the weapon, held it high above his head and let out a shrill whoop. His celebration was interrupted by the sound of horse hooves on the road. Thinking his companions were leaving, he dropped the pitchfork and went to the door. Suddenly there was musket fire near the house, a dozen or so shots. As the lone renegade watched a cavalry troop cut down his brothers, eight-year-old Lavinia crawled from under the straw, picked up the pitchfork and jammed it into the back of the kill-er's neck. The man sunk to his knees and then fell face down onto the barn floor. The child walked to the doorway and stood over her kill like a Celtic warrior, victorious in battle. Blood trickled from the back of the renegade's neck onto his cheek and into his glossed-over left eye. She spat on the man much like she had seen her father do when he was angry about something.

When the musket smoke had dissipated from around the house and the other Indians lay dead in the front yard, Lavinia staggered back to her brother's body. His bright red blood had now soaked into the hay. Dropping to her knees, she sobbed bitterly. In a few minutes, a large Army sergeant stepped into the barn, checked the Indian for life, then gently took the diminutive Lavinia into his arms.

After helping her gather some belongings from the house, the sergeant hoisted her onto the buckboard seat. She held a rag doll close into her body and scooted over to allow the soldier to sit beside her. As he clicked his tongue and slapped the reins onto the horse's backside, the wagon pulled away. She did not take her eyes off the three mounds of fresh dirt that lay beneath the large oak on which the bodies of five mutilated renegades hung.

Lavinia opened her eyes and the tears came again, as they had for nearly twenty years of gloomy days, just like this one.

Peeples awoke to something jabbing him sharply in the ribs. Where was he? Did he just have the worst nightmare of his life? Then the horror of the night before re-entered his brain. Not a dream. It was all too real. Standing over Peeples was a man with a nightstick in his hands. "We have vagrancy laws in this town, mister."

"Who the devil are you?' Peeples asked, sitting upright, then suddenly feeling the stiffness in his back and soreness in his ribs.

"I am Officer Jacob Lively, Charleston constable. I will put the same question to you….who the devil are *you*?

"Officer, I am most pleased to see you. As a matter of fact, I am pleased to be seeing anything."

Lively appeared puzzled, especially when Peeples asked the officer to escort him to the city jail. "Name is Peeples, sir, and I must report an attempt on my life."

Margaret Cleary, a stately and handsome woman with high cheek bones and superbly-coifed auburn hair, kissed her husband on the cheek as he buttoned the last fastener on his vest in front of the mirror. He was ever conscious of his appearance, not for reasons of vanity, but because he felt it important for a city official to look his professional best. Much unlike the uncouth, unkempt Chauncey Harriman. Cleary was an elegant dresser whose clothes always looked immaculate and pressed in spite of the thick and heavy humidity. Moreover, he was the perfect placidity of temperament; a temperament as polished as his wit.

"You are a most dignified man, Colonel Cleary" she said, straightening his collar and adjusting his sash. "I should be concerned about the women in this town when you appear on the street. I see the way Frances Worthington tosses her pretty head around and flutters her eyelashes. She says 'Oh, Nate, won't you stop in for one of my pastries? I made a lemon tart especially for you today.'"

"Now, Margaret. You know the woman has eaten too many of her own fancy baked goods. A pretty face, perhaps, but she only wishes she had your figure. I expect she probably killed off Mister Worthington with the lard she puts into her wares. I will be sure to get my sweets at home, my dear." Cleary smiled and patted her behind.

A knock at the door interrupted the Cleary's playful tete-a-tete. Margaret went to the front door, finding Miller. He quickly removed his hat and bowed as she let him in. "Good day, Madam Cleary. You're looking most lovely today."

"You are too kind, Mister Miller. You are mighty dapper yourself. I suppose you're here for my husband.' She turned toward the bedroom. "Nate!"

Cleary, who had shoved his pistol into the sash near the front of his left leg, strode into the hallway. "What is it, Miller? Is there something that could not wait until I arrived at the jail?"

"There is a matter of importance awaiting you, Chief Constable." He looked toward Margaret, hesitating to continue.

"It is all right, Miller. Whatever the business, Mrs. Cleary has heard much these years living with me."

The constable nodded and began again. "It seems a traveler has narrowly escaped our friends at Six Mile House who plotted his murder last evening. The man managed to get away and was found at St. Michael's this morning. He is most shaken, sir, but eager to convey to you his story."

"Then we will go." The chief kissed his wife on her forehead and led Miller out of the house. "The Fishers, ay? Did I not tell you something was amiss with that woman?"

Miller nodded like an obedient child and took a seat beside Cleary in the carriage.

"Sit down, young man. What is your story?'

Peeples began the incredible account of his near murder. Cleary sat expressionless, taking notes and occasionally glancing at Miller, who stood wide-eyed, shaking his head in disbelief. Cleary's confirming eyes validated his intuition about Lavinia Fisher, and Miller sheepishly realized how the woman could so blind a man with her beauty and charm, including him.

Cleary rested his elbows on the desk, interlocked his fingers and positioned his chin on his hands in reflection. "I expect we will soon find Mr. Hastings, Malcolm." Miller nodded.

As Constable Jacob Lively had the reputation as the city's 'town crier', he had already parlayed the news of the bizarre night to his friends from the tavern. Only minutes after discharging Peeples to Miller at the city jail, he was at David Ross' house filling him in on the details. Acting in the fashion of a Paul Revere, Ross then rode to the houses and businesses of his friends, summoning them to meet at the dock at the end of Meeting Street. Finally they had the goods on the Fisher gang. Today they would be the surrogates of justice and evoke the Lynch Law.

Ross would lead the posse as he had vowed months before. They would start with Five Mile House, where all of the gang was said to nest. All except the Fishers. The cavaliers would capture or kill as necessary and burn the house down. Then they would move on to Six Mile for the Fishers. With fire in their bellies and grit in their jaws, eight horsemen, armed to the teeth, thundered across the Ashley Bridge just after ten-thirty. Ross set the gallop pace to the front of the pack.

As some of the vigilantes realized there was no defined plan of attack for the raid, one of the men, Corey Raines, called for a halt only two miles out of the city. "What the devil are we to do when we reach Five Mile, Ross? Do we just ride upon the place and storm the house? What if they see us? We may get ambushed."

Finch interjected, "No. We just ride in there and torch the place. The element of surprise, mate. They ain't expectin' us and we'll be on 'em like a swarm of bees before they know what's happenin.'"

Ross could see some dissention in the ranks and he tried to head it off before he lost control of his men. "Look, boys, we'll just ride upon the house, surround it and call them out. If they start shooting, we'll shoot the place up and then burn it to the ground."

"I don't know, Ross," replied Raines. "Maybe we should have just let the police handle the matter. We all got charged up back there in town and didn't think it all through. What we're doin' here is against the law."

"If any of you are not with me on this," said Ross, "then you are free to turn back." There was a new and different tone of anger in his voice. He had hoped to shame anyone who did not have the courage to continue on.

Three men, including Raines, mumbled among themselves, shook their heads and gave Ross their looks of retreat. "We're going back, Ross. Mason here has a new child and doesn't want to risk injury or death doin' the work of the law."

"Then be off with you!" Ross cast him a look of disdain, then turned his head toward the others. "Are you with me or not?"

Another man turned his horse to join the three deserters. Split evenly, the two groups of horsemen parted ways, one toward the north and the other toward the city. Now Ross, Fletcher, Finch and the fourth man, James Callison, faced different odds. The time for reckless abandon was over. Ross had to come up with a new plan. Finch and Fletcher were sharpshooters, but if they were out-manned and out-gunned, accuracy mattered very little. If they did run into a hail of bullets and were routed, they would split up and reconsolidate on the city side of the Ashley Bridge.

At a vantage point where they wouldn't be detected, but still having a view of Five Mile House, Ross and his troop set up well back in the thicket. "Fletcher and I will casually ride upon the house as though we might be visitors, but Avery, you and James ride around that tree line on the left and set up in the back to rush the house from the rear. If any shootin' starts or anyone runs out the back, then let 'em have it."

As instructed, James Callison and Avery Finch rode off into the trees on the left and after an agreed-to five minutes, Ross and Fletcher prepared to move out of the bush. Suddenly, two riders approached from Old Dorchester way, trotting their horses into the front yard of the house. "Wait," whispered Ross. "I recognize one of them. The fella in the brown coat is Darrell Johnson. That one's mean as a snake."

After tying off his horse at the hitch rail, Johnson grabbed his partner Stewart's arm. "Did you see that? Look yonder by the tree line in back of the house. Two riders movin' in." In posturing to set up at the rear of Five Mile House, Callison and Finch had failed to take notice of the two approaching gang members.

When Ross saw Johnson and Stewart running to retrieve their muskets from the flanks of their horses, he led the charge from the woods. He and Fletcher bolted onto the two men before they could take up positions. Johnson fired in the direction of Ross. Fletcher pulled up his horse to an abrupt stop, rested the barrel of his rifle on his left arm and exploded a mini-ball into Johnson's throat. The man, already dead on his feet, spiraled into the porch railing and plunged face down into the earth. Stewart immediately dropped his rifle and threw his hands into the air.

After the vigilantes searched the house, finding no one else, they bound Stewart with ropes and flung him over his saddle. Ross found some oily rags in the house, struck a match to them and tossed them onto the porch. Within two minutes the front of the house was ablaze and in twenty, the remainder of the tinderbox was entirely engulfed. Flames shot forty feet into the air, catching the branches of a nearby willow. The heat was so intense, the men backed their horses up to the road. For more than a half-hour they sat stoically on their mounts until the second floor fell into the first.

Unbeknownst to Ross, three other friends of John Fisher, namely Joe Roberts, Seth Young and James Sterritt, had set up in proximity to Five Mile House, poised to prey on unsuspecting travelers. When they heard the shot that felled Johnson, they walked their horses with stealth to peer through the trees just off the Dorchester. Witnessing the torching of their hideout, they scurried off to Six Mile to warn the Fishers.

A few minutes later, the vigilantes moved onto Six Mile Inn. This time Ross, spurred by his triumph at Five Mile, brazenly dismounted at the gate. With the three rifles of his men trained on the front of the house, he stepped onto the porch and began beating on the door. Suddenly, from the rear of the house Roberts and the others seized upon the vigilante party, firing volleys of shots that dropped Fletcher from his saddle and struck Finch in the shoulder. Ross made it to his horse, but was grazed by a bullet in his thigh. Callison and the wounded Finch wheeled their horses around and accelerated into a gallop with the gang on their heels, leaving Ross and Fletcher behind. The front door opened and Fisher appeared with a pistol, firing a shot that whizzed innocently past Ross' head. Ross managed to get to Fletcher and help him onto his horse. As the plan was foiled, both riders broke for the woods to avoid the advancing Seth Young, who had turned back his mount to finish them off.

Broken in body and spirit from the imbroglio, Ross and his men split in two directions, somehow managing to successfully evade their pursuers. After searching the woods for the vigilantes, the highway gang gave up the chase. Not because they gave up heart, but because they spied from the thicket the three carriages of constables commanded by Colonel Cleary on the road toward Six Mile House.

Fisher listened from the porch for any continuing sounds of the skirmish, but apparently the combatants were out of earshot. The door opened behind him and Lavinia appeared with the musket from the mantle in hand.

"I feared that someday someone would come and try taking Six Mile," she said. "It was a matter of time they would connect the robberies on the road with us."

"They have no way of knowing that, Lavinia. All of us had our faces covered in the robberies. I see no way anyone could have tied us in. Just because the hold-ups occurred between here and Five Mile don't give cause for people to say we were involved."

"Until now. Our ambush of that raiding party will definitely bring the law out here. It won't take a genius to figure it out."

Fisher led Lavinia back inside. He took a half-smoked stogie from his breast pocket and jammed it unlit into his mouth. "Something else brought that bunch out here. I know Ross has been tryin' to get his hands on this place for years, but I can't believe that was their reason for the raid."

"May be," replied Lavinia. "Perhaps they *have* someway connected us to the highway gang and Ross used the information as a ploy to raid us and take over the house. I'm just puzzled as to why the law didn't act on it if there was any proof. There's definitely something else. Something we haven't thought about. I've got a bad feeling about this, John. Now the law *will* be down on us after that shootout. I'm thinking we need to lock this place up for a while and head out of state. Maybe down to Savannah."

"Nah. Don't worry your pretty head, darlin'. We were just protectin' our place that's all. Who can fault us with beatin' off a bunch of outlaws who just burnt one place and was tryin' to take ours?"

Lavinia, who was still standing at the dining room window watching out for a possible reprisal from the raiders, nodded her head and said, "We are soon to find out, my husband. Yonder comes Mr. Cleary."

Upon dismounting, two constables ran to the rear of the inn and another scurried to the barn as Cleary and Miller ascended the front porch steps. Cleary rapped on the door with the butt of his pistol and called out. "Madam Fisher, are you inside?"

Within moments the door opened and Lavinia's wanly face appeared. "Good day, Mr. Cleary," she replied in a nervous voice, but still offering up her radiant smile. She was remarkably stunning in her gingham print dress and sweeping black hair held impeccably kempt by the tortoise-shell combs.

"You do know why we are here, Mrs. Fisher?" asked Cleary. She did not immediately respond, but swallowed hard behind her smile.

"I assume you have been chasing a band of robbers and vandals. They attacked our home and I have word that they burnt a house down the road."

Cleary stood erect with the pistol now down by his side and eyed her sternly. "Where is your husband, madam?"

The inadvertent turn of her head in the direction of the guestroom gave his position away. Miller moved swiftly into the room, allowing his gun to lead the way, and found John Fisher cowering in a corner behind the six-foot wardrobe.

Lavinia started to utter something, perhaps in protest of Miller's advance upon her husband, but then turned back to the chief. "Why have you descended upon us, sir? We are the ones who were assaulted."

"I know nothing about a band of robbers, although two of my men have gone to the house at Five Mile to see about the fire."

From behind his back he produced a pair of shackles and placed them on her small wrists. "Lavinia Fisher, I place you under arrest for the attempted murder of John Peeples and as a suspect in the disappearance of William Hastings."

Her smile was replaced by a mouth drawn in terror. "Attempted murder? And what's this about the man named Hastings?" She summoned from her dramatic repertoire a look of confusion and bewilderment.

"Mr. Peeples is alive and well, Mrs. Fisher. And if you will check the pit beneath your guest's bed, you will find only his bedcovers."

Lavinia continued her façade of innocence. But then the reality that somehow Peeples was not in the cellar stunned her. He had escaped? She looked away, far away, through the walls and into another dimension. After a moment, she turned a resigned face back to Cleary's steely eyes. "I did like Mr. Peeples and am glad he is alive." She paused a moment and her smile returned, but faintly so. "May I offer you a cup of tea, Mr. Cleary?"

He couldn't tell whether this was a serious offer. Perhaps in realizing he knew about the poison potion, she was just being sardonic. Lavinia's eyes now fully reflected her guilt. Cleary was relentless in his stare.

"Where is the man known as Heyward?"

"I am not sure, sir. He left at first light," she replied. "I very much do not like the man and will gladly tell you where he lives."

At that moment, Miller came out with the shackled John Fisher. "He was lying in a corner like a terrified rat and surrendered without as much a whimper, Chief Constable."

Lavinia looked in disgust at her husband's pitiful demeanor. His lips were quivering, his body appearing as a puppet, limp and manipulated. Staring with disdain at the slumping figure, she said "You will find my husband's friend, Heyward, in a shack near Moore's Landing. As he is such a louse, Heyward will already be drunk at this hour, so he will give you no fight." John raised his sulking head to give Lavinia a look of contempt. It wasn't enough *they* were in hot water; she had betrayed his friend as well.

As the constables guarded the prisoners on the veranda, Cleary and Miller entered the guestroom described by Peeples. On the surface the room was neat and homey. The bed looked inviting, like it would give any weary wayfarer a most restful night of sleep. But how many guests had met their end on this mattress? If Peeples was not the first victim, how many other men had gone missing from their families at the hands of John and Lavinia Fisher? How many others had she poisoned with her special tea? Cleary was ready to find out.

He found the latches on the flooring beneath the bed, just as Peeples had related. Running his hand along the wall behind the bed, he also discovered the lever. As Miller unbolted the floor latches, Cleary pulled the lever. Suddenly the bed and floor swung away, exposing the rectangular hole that led to the cellar. Immediately, the stench of rotting flesh filled the room, gagging the visitors and compelling them to apply handkerchiefs to their noses and mouths.

Cleary took a moment to regain his composure, then spotting a lantern on the dresser, he lit its wick. Again he drew in a deep breath through his handkerchief and swallowed the putrid acid that had pumped to his throat. As he lowered the light into the hole, he was truly not prepared for what he would find. The scene was grotesque beyond human sanity. He turned his head away, momentarily, trying again to control his stomach. Miller's retching was not helping. On the dirt floor of the cellar lay the corpse of a half-skeletal man atop the bones and clothing of what appeared to be three or four other human remains. Cleary would have to bring the coroner and a grave detail back to the inn to pull out the remains to assess the actual numbers of bodies and their identities. Scattered onto and around the corpses was a white powder, perhaps lye, which would accelerate the decomposition and aid in keeping much of the decaying odor within the cellar.

At Cleary's direction, Miller assisted him in pulling the bed and floor back into place, re-locking the bolts. Other men would have to deal with this horror, but Cleary would certainly deal with the murderers. As he walked back onto the porch, he avoided eye contact with the Fishers. "Get them out of here," he barked to his officers.

Lavinia descended the steps with a constable's grip on her arm, then stopped for a moment to pinch off an errant vine from the delicate bourgainvilles that twined around the portico. Before moving on, she took a long last look at the short row of white tombstones in the small family graveyard. For years now she could not remember the faces of her parents and brother, and this had always haunted her. As she looked back at her beloved house, the officer nudged her on. Along the flagstone walkway she held her head high with all the poise and grace of a Charleston socialite. The days ahead would be difficult and she would have to cultivate as much strength and dignity as she could muster in meeting her impending fate.

CHAPTER EIGHT

On the way back to Charleston, two of the constables diverted to the west and onto Amelia Road to Moore's Landing, where they found Heyward passed out in a state of intoxication, just as Lavinia had predicted. Only an hour before, he had returned from the market where he sold a side of rustled beef and downed a quart of rye to celebrate. As they had trouble rousting him, he was handcuffed and carried in a comatose condition to the officers' buckboard.

Cleary unshackled Lavinia's wrists, allowed her to walk on her own into the cell and clanked the door shut behind him. He turned to walk away without word, but stopped short, pausing for a few seconds with his back to her, then wheeled around to look at her. She stood in the center of the eight by eight room which was lit only by a small, barred window.

"There are some things in this life I cannot fathom; and this, madam, by far outweighs them all. You live in a lovely inn, manage a comfortable lifestyle and have a degree of culture about you, and are quite possibly the most beautiful woman I have ever seen. How could you perpetrate such a grizzly series of crimes?"

Lavinia moved gracefully to the cell door and placed her hands on the bars. "Sir, it seems you have already convicted me before my trial. Did we not address such matters in our constitution some forty years ago?"

"Don't be insolent, Mrs. Fisher. Yes, you are merely charged with these heinous murders, but I have seen the evidence and it is surely not in your favor. There is no possible way you can explain away what we discovered. You will indeed get a trial, and I personally will see that it is a fair one; but I must say with my experience, you will not overcome this evidence."

She placed her hands on her hips and glared at Cleary, but had no retort. Her eyes said it all. But then she softened and said "Would you be so kind to contact John Heath on Broad Street by the dry goods store and ask him if he would consider representing my husband and me?"

"Madam, I know of Mr. Heath and he completed the law school only a year ago. He has not had so much as three cases and these involved petty crimes. He seems a very fine and eager young man, but would you not be better served by one with considerably more experience?"

"Perhaps, sir, but he was in my school when I was a young girl and we were friends. I am sure he will represent me with competence."

Cleary nodded. "Very well, Mrs. Fisher. I will also have my wife come by occasionally to see to your special needs." He turned and made his way up the stairs of the Old Jail to his office on the main floor.

Lavinia's new quarters contained only a cot with soiled sheets and a mangy blanket, a toilet pot and a wash basin coated with black and green scum. The entire dungeon smelled of mildew and urine. The only women who had ever occupied these cells were prostitutes and runaway slaves. This particular cell was generally reserved for a woman, primarily because it had a bed; however, the rat-infested guestroom was still an unfit accommodation for any human, much less a woman. But at least her cell had a floor. There were nine other units on the ground floor series of dungeon cells with dirt floors and mainly occupied by drunken seamen, vagrants and other vermin.

As Lavinia sat quietly on her cot, hands folded and head down, she heard a chorus of catcalls, snoring and bellowing echoing throughout the dungeon gangway. The man in the cell next to her appeared to be afflicted with consumption, making gagging and hacking sounds as he coughed. 'Where had they put John?' she wondered. He was not incarcerated on her level. She missed him. And she missed Six Mile House, her bed, and her beautiful flower garden. She sobbed, bitterly. There was no way she could endure the horror and decadence of such a place. When night came, noises from the other cells and the business of the rats would be magnified. She would be in holy terror. Lavinia would rather take her own life and taste the fires of Hell for all eternity than spend a week in this cesspool.

When Cleary opened the door to his office, he was surprised to see his nemesis, Chauncey Harriman, sitting at his desk. The man hadn't been to the Old Jail, even on official business, in at least two years.

"I must congratulate you on your apprehension of these killers today, Cleary," he said wryly. "But I presume if it had not been for Peeples coming to you about the Fishers, you would still be chasing your tail around the city. I suppose even a blind hog can occasionally find a truffle in a pile of dung." He chuckled at his attempt to be witty.

Cleary felt his neck burning under his collar, but held his tongue. Harriman was a reptile, all right…slimy, bug-eyed and repulsive. The chief fully expected the man to flick his tongue out some day and knock down a fly.

"She will have John Heath to represent her," said Cleary. "I do not know if he will take the husband's case as well, but expect so."

"Heath?" the magistrate laughed. His enlarged stomach shook like warm fat. "If he will represent the Fishers, we should start building the gallows as we speak. He insults the law with his incompetence. Why, he has only had a handful of cases, and as I remember, did his clients much disservice."

"Just the same, I am bound to approach the man on her behalf."

Harriman rose to his feet from Cleary's chair. "As Judge Bay and I will preside over this matter, I look forward to the boob embarrassing himself."

By dusk, the news of the arrests had spread throughout Charleston like a prairie fire. As there had been a social bitterness between Lavinia and the aristocratic women of the city, the tongue waggers reminded one another they suspected that this woman was involved in some illicit scheme, but never dreamed it would be murder. The men of Charleston who patronized the pubs and taverns, whether affluent or lowly in status, were aghast that such a beautiful and charming young woman would ever be capable of committing such atrocities. Surely it was all a mistake or some conspiracy.

Matthew Cowher was stunned. Upon hearing the report from his secretary, he went to the altar and fell on his knees to pray for Lavinia's well-being and the deliverance of her soul. She might be a child of darkness, as she called herself, but she could be no murderess.

"Father in Heaven,' he cried out. "I beseech Ye to bless and protect my young friend in her plight. I pray that the case made against her is untrue and that she will come from the matter, unscathed and vindicated. Give her strength and resolve to bear what lies before her. Unleash Thy merciful and celestial power to take this burden away from Lavinia and put her on the path of righteousness, so that she may indeed feel the warmth of Your light. Grant to her Your mercy and give her peace, and I will give Thee all the praise to which You are entitled. In the name of He who is most precious, Thy Son Christ Jesus. Amen and amen."

Matthew remained on his knees, hands under his chin and fingers interlocked, for several minutes, with no other words in his head, numb and emotionally wasted.

It was now raining a cold rain. Cleary was still in his office at six to assure that all prisoners were fed when Matthew arrived. The platters had been prepared with pork, beans and bread, barely fit for human consumption. Generally, what scraps were left over from the boarding house restaurant on Broad Street the day before were retrieved by one of the constables and apportioned out for each prisoner.

The chief stood in respect when the minister entered the room. "Good evening, Parson."

Matthew nodded and extended his hand to Cleary. "And good day to you, Chief Constable. I trust this dreary evening finds you well. How is Margaret?"

Cleary smiled and replied "As doting as ever, Matthew. I can scarcely finish dressing in the morning that she doesn't put me through some kind of regimental inspection, preparing me for my appearance to the world. But she is a dear woman and I am fortunate to be her husband."

"She is indeed a blessing to everyone, Nathaniel. And one of the pillars of our church."

"As you have been here on numerous occasions to minister to the poor souls in this lovely boarding house, Matthew, I have the notion you are not here for any of the usual riff-raff."

The minister nodded.

"She is in the cell directly at the bottom of the stairs. If you are so inclined, you may take this platter to her. As you are a man of God, I am trusting you bear no weapons."

Matthew gave him a momentary look of consternation, which prompted the Chief to apologize. "Sorry, Matthew. It is only my position that compelled me to mention that. Not my heart."

"I would not be offended if you searched me, Nathaniel. You know there are men more prominent than me in this community who would not be above reproach in a matter such as this. You are certainly aware of my fondness for Mrs. Fisher."

"I know that you looked after her when she was a child. I remember seeing her on the street with you and your assistant twenty or so years ago after her parents were killed. I have also known you these many years to be nothing less than honorable. A search will not be necessary."

Matthew bowed respectfully, took the tray from the Chief, then proceeded down the brick stairs.

It nearly broke his heart to see Lavinia in the dungeon cell, sitting on the bed, head in hands. His footsteps startled her and as it was dark throughout the corridor, she did not immediately recognize him. When his face finally came into view by the waning light of day that streamed through the barred window, she turned her head away. "I wish no dinner nor any conversation with you, Matthew."

He pulled a chair from its place against the stone wall and drew it close to the bars, but did not sit down. "We must talk, Lavinia. I find these charges difficult to believe and insist you tell me they are false."

Lavinia turned her head back to him and then after a moment stood and walked to the cell door. He could now see her more clearly and that her beautiful eyes were red and swollen. The eyes darted back and forth into his. It was as though she was waiting for the right words to come out.

"I cannot, Matthew. Whatever I have become, I cannot find it in my heart to ever lie to you."

Matthew dropped his head in disbelief, then reached through the bars to put her hands in his. "Then it is all true."

She paused, but kept her eyes unwavering on his. "Yes," she said softly.

Tears welled in his eyes. "My God, Lavinia. Why?" She squeezed his hands and stood looking dejected for a moment, then responded. "I have told you, Matthew, that there were things you did not know about me. Evil has lain on my heart for so long that it has become a part of me as much as my arms and legs. As your God directs you to be a righteous man, so is the devil my bedfellow. The day your God allowed my family to be murdered was the day I lost my soul. If you are here to help this child of darkness find it, then you are a fool."

"It grieves me to hear you speak these things. I ask that you repent of your sins now, here, before the Almighty. He will forgive you, Lavinia. Whatever you have done, He will forgive you. And so will I."

"Go away, Matthew. Do not waste your time on a doomed woman."

He brought her hands to his mouth and touched them to his lips. As he did so, he prayed a silent prayer, then after a moment, released them. He looked again into her sad eyes and turned to leave without a word. Matthew's tears had now blinded him, making it difficult for him to negotiate the steps. He tripped on one of the bricks, badly bruising his shin. But the pain he felt in his leg paled in comparison to the injury to his heart.

The remnants of Ross' vigilante party met as originally planned near the Ashley Bridge and gathered around eight that evening at the Dock Street Tavern to reconstitute. Fletcher was still in the hospital with a bullet in his side, but Finch and Ross had been patched up and released. Lamenting their failed mission to take Six Mile, they consumed several tankards of ale to address the pain of their wounded bodies and egos. As word had also traveled about town regarding their plight as well as the capture of the Fishers, their whereabouts were easily learned by Roberts and his accomplices. Having a little too much drink and too little fight, Ross and his cohorts were lay-wasted outside of the tavern. Ross was beaten severely and tossed through the tavern's window. Finch sustained another wound, this time from the business side of a knife, and Callison was nearly kicked to death. Two constables who had happened nearby gave chase to the gang, taking down only Roberts. John Fisher now had a cellmate.

Dr. Jervis Henry Stevens, the city's coroner, a bespectacled, balding man in his mid-sixties, allowed nearly all other men to tower over him, standing at barely five feet. At around nine-thirty on the nineteenth he accompanied Cleary and a grave detail to Six Mile House to retrieve and examine the bodies beneath the flooring. As Cleary nosed around in the kitchen area gathering samples of the tea and a metal can containing what appeared to be the poisonous powder, Dr. Stevens and his helpers broke down an outside door to the cellar that had been sealed off years before. Carefully, they gathered what was left of a man estimated to be dead four or five months and the clothed bones of four other humans, carrying them out of the cellar and laying them side by side on the grass. From the pants pocket of the most recent corpse, Stevens secured a paper containing the names of William Hastings and Benjamin Farthmore.

"Chief Cleary!" Stevens called into the house. "We have Mr. Hastings here."

Cleary joined the coroner in the yard and said "How can you be sure, Dr. Stevens?"

The doctor showed the chief the paper. "Here is something else his murderers failed to take from him, probably in their haste to dispose of the body." On a nearly fully decayed finger was a gold signet ring with the initials *W.H.* "It would be improbable, given the paper, approximate date of his demise and the ring, that this is not Mr. Hastings."

"I would agree, sir," replied Cleary. "Is there any way to identify the other skeletal remains?" He winced as though he were in pain when he scanned the corpses.

"At this point, no. There are no papers among the clothes and bones. The lye has done its job as much of the clothing has deteriorated along with the flesh. But identities or not, you have more than enough evidence here to see their ruthless killers swing from the gallows."

"Yes." Cleary nodded and sighed. "I must agree."

After climbing the flight of stairs and taking inventory of three of the rooms on the upper level the Chief Constable entered the Fishers' quarters. He was immediately taken aback, even stunned. It was beyond him that a woman who kept such a tasteful and aesthetic bedroom, punctuated with Old World, artisan furniture and fashionable drapes, could be nothing but a rogue criminal…a robber and a murderess. Now devoid of the stench of rotting flesh two levels down, he took into his nostrils a pleasant aroma. The room smelled like her. Like the hand that he had kissed on his first visit to the inn.

On a trunk at the foot of their bed Cleary spied two pieces of cloth: one made of burlap and one of a more flimsy material. He examined them, taking note of the two holes in each. Masks. Lifting the lighter one to his nose, he nodded. It was her smell. Her lilac water. Now he had evidence that the Fishers were also the two bandits that had been lay-wasting merchants upon the pike. He would add this to the more grievous murder charges.

Three days later, upon learning that intruders were seen carrying off furniture and other items from Six Mile House, Cleary and another constable dispatched to the inn to board it up. As it had not taken long for the locals to learn the place was unoccupied, vagrants and thieves had begun cleaning out the premises. Gone were Lavinia's precious English china, pieces of fine furniture, food and liquor, clothing and personal articles. If the police had not arrived when they did, the house would have been little more than a shell. Upon inspecting the barn, the officers found that the Fishers' beautiful roan and cow were stolen as well. Someone had even taken the crusty old steer from the meadow. Finding two dozen 6 foot yellow-pine planks and some nails, the constables proceeded to board up all doors and windows on the house and barn.

Knowing Cleary was at Six Mile that morning, Chauncey Harriman paid a visit to the Old Jail. Only a neophyte constable remained on duty at the jail, but when the magistrate asked for a key to her cell, the young officer was astute enough to ask Harriman what his intentions were.

"To gather information for her trial, you half-wit."

"But sir, I have orders from the Chief Constable to let no one enter her cell. I don't pretend to know much about the law, but should the judge trying a prisoner's case be talking to her?

Harriman placed his hands on his thick sides and pushed his reddened face into the constable's. "How dare a lowly police-man such as you tell me my business or question the authority or purpose of my high office! Now hand me the key or by nightfall you will no longer wear that badge."

Intimidated and speechless, the jailer reluctantly held out the set of keys, which Harriman snatched angrily from his hand. Giving the officer one last sneer, he turned and made his way toward the stairs. As it was rather dark, the magistrate negotiated the steps carefully. Lavinia saw the outline of a large form groping its way along the wall, then heard a man mumble something about "this deplorable dung hole." When he reached the bottom of the steps he called out "Lavinia Fisher! I will have a word with you."

Still not able to fully discern the man's identity, she asked, "Who is there?" in a small voice.

"The man who will hold your very life in his hands," he replied. His face now came into view from the window light.

"What do you want, sir?"

"I will ask the questions, but if you must know, to discuss with you the constable's findings at your inn." As there were several keys on the ring, Harriman tried five in the lock before hearing it click.

Lavinia jumped up from her cot and ran to the back wall when the door swung open.

"Sir, you are not my lawyer and you of all people should not be here. I will scream."

"Go ahead, lassie. Scream to your heart's desire. No one will hear you down here. Now come away from the wall and sit on the bed."

"No, I will not! Now leave at once!" Lavinia began to shake.

Harriman approached her and stood within inches from her body. "Listen, girly. Your cooperation will determine whether or not I hang that husband of yours as soon as I leave this cell. Maybe I'll drag you to the gallows as well." He placed a large clammy hand on her wrist, then jerked her away from the wall and onto the bed. Planting his right knee into the cot, he eased his large frame onto her body.

Lavinia clenched her fists and pushed into his chest to separate their bodies. But the man was too strong. As she flailed away at him, he massaged her breast with one paw and grabbed a handful of pinned-up hair with the other. The tortoise shell combs fell away as her silken black hair dropped to her shoulders.

Harriman put his face against hers and said "You will not be insolent with me, little witch. I think you know what I mean by your cooperation." He then clamped his grotesque lips onto hers and put his hand inside her petticoat between her legs. Moaning, he began to unbutton his trousers.

Lavinia clawed at his face with her razor-like nails, nearly separating his eyeball from its socket. Harriman yelled out in pain, then slapped her hard across the face. As the bed was close up against the cell's bars, her head struck one of them. Dazed and helpless, heart in her throat, she found that she could not cry out. The fat man fumbled inside the trouser flap to take out his member, raised her dress, then positioned his two hundred fifty-pound frame onto her body. Lavinia finally managed to scream and called for Cleary.

"He won't hear you. He is busy at your inn, gathering more evidence for your hanging," Harriman said, licking her lips as though she were succulent pork ribs. "Just let it happen, Lavinia. This may be the last pleasure you will experience before I snap your neck at the gallows." He laughed and drooled onto her dress.

She spat in his face, wanting to vomit from the foul odor of his breath. As the massive blubber in his lower stomach was interfering with his ability to enter her, he used his right hand to re-arrange his genitals. Harriman tore away her pantaloons, then grabbed one of the cell bars to steady himself on her tiny body, poised to thrust.

Suddenly, there was click in his ear. When he raised his head from Lavinia's face he found himself staring down the barrel of a cocked pistol.

"You contemptible sack of horse dung. Get off the woman, now, or the ball inside of this pistol will splatter your brains onto the far wall!"

Harriman rolled off of Lavinia and landed on the floor. Shoving his genitals inside his pants, he cowered into a large ball against the cell wall. "Please be careful with that, madam, or it may go off accidentally."

Margaret Cleary continued to train the piece onto his head. "If it goes off, it will not be by accident."

"Please, Margaret," the magistrate pleaded, shielding his face with an arm. "Please have mercy. I know this was wrong, but you know..." He gulped. "You know how I am. Just...just please lower the weapon."

Another figure moved in behind Margaret and she turned her head to see the face of her husband.

"I'll take over now, my dear," Cleary said, lifting the pistol from her hand. "You should have shot the bastard." He then turned his attention to the pathetic creature on the floor. "Get on your feet, Judge Harriman. Get the hell out of this building and do not feign to ever have business here again. If you do not heed my words, judge or not, I will arrest you and throw you into the worst of these cells. It will be a fitting home for the rat that you are."

Harriman, apparently regaining just an inkling of courage and dignity, picked himself up and thrust out his chin while refastening his trousers. "You have not heard the last of this Cleary. You have threatened me and insulted my office. This very day, I will go to work having you replaced."

"It is you who degrades and defiles your own office. Now **go!**" Cleary commanded, swinging the pistol back in the magistrate's direction and training it on the man's privates. This prompted the big man to turn and double time up the steps, making sure he cleared the top landing out of sight before yelling back "Mark my words, Cleary. You will be out in the street by year's end!"

"Did he hurt you?" the Chief asked Lavinia.

"I am fine, sir" she said, wiping blood from her lips. She then looked through the bars at Margaret. "Thank you, ma'am, for stopping him."

She nodded a welcome, but without emotion. "'A most horrid man, that one."

Margaret may have stopped Lavinia's rape, but she was still abhorred at the thought of this woman murdering all those poor men. Cleary shoved the pistol into his belt and led Margaret by her waist up the long stairwell.

Lavinia lay back onto the cot and pressed her lip hard against the sheet to stop the bleeding. If the man had completed his rape, she would have asked Cleary for the pistol and ended her life this very day.

CHAPTER NINE

John Davis Heath, in practice scarcely a year, was taken in as a junior associate by long-time legal icon, Christopher Mellon. Seven months later, Mellon fell dead of heart failure into his plate of ham and eggs at Samuel Giddings, a popular restaurant catering to prominent citizens, politicians and lawyers. Heath suddenly found himself partnered with Mellon's son, Jake, another young neophyte attorney. Mellon and Heath, P.A. struggled to gain the confidence of the populace, many of whom had withdrawn to other firms staffed with more seasoned and reputable attorneys. In June of that year, Mellon gave up his share of the practice to Heath, leaving him with the store front office and, of course, the rent.

Davey Heath, as he was known by his friends, was a nice-looking young man, still single, not particularly handsome, but always well dressed and groomed and wearing an intelligent sparkle in his eye. As he and Lavinia were schoolmates, they had remained friends these dozen years. He had been to Six Mile House several times, twice for dinner, but mostly it was Lavinia who dropped by his office three or four times a year for some friendly conversation. Heath was probably the only man of whom John Fisher was not jealous. Perhaps it was Davey's delicate manner or his Old Charleston refinement that gave Fisher the impression that he preferred the men. Of course, by convincing him that each of Lavinia's few male friends were powder puffs and had no vital capacity for the ladies, it allowed him to better deal with his jealousy issues.

As summoned, Heath met with the accused individually, basically informing them that since the evidence was so overwhelming and incriminating, they should consider a plea for mercy. This, however, realistically meant no mercy in Hanging Harry's courtroom. As Heath was assured that each of his clients would face the gallows, he intended to drag out the process so that his clients would have more days to live and make things right with God.

Lavinia had little to say to Heath, but expressed that she was glad he was there for her. John, on the other hand vehemently denied ever killing anyone. Heath shook his head sadly and as much told him that if Lavinia was found guilty, the court would find him guilty as a conspirator. No man would believe the husband was not just as guilty. Although he may never have put poison in a cup of tea or pulled the trigger on a man, it was obvious he did conspire along with his wife and disposed of the bodies. There was little Heath could do for John; however, he proposed to both him and Lavinia that the defense be split. He would represent Lavinia and a fellow attorney put on a separate defense for John.

"Why would you do that, Davey?" she asked.

"I have some ideas about your case, Lavinia. I think it would serve us well to play on the jury's sympathy in your case. No man wants to see a woman put to death. And if I can show that your husband, a man with a history of questionable repute, so tragically influenced you, perhaps they would see fit to be lenient with you. Of course that would leave my more experienced counterpart the unenviable task of putting on a hopeless case for John."

"I certainly don't wish to hang for whatever I am accused of doing, but I will not give up John nor allow you to put on such a defense that will in essence send John to the gallows."

"It wouldn't be like that, Lavinia. I would collaborate with his counsel to come up with a joint defense that would hopefully place questions in the minds of the jurors. Questions as to whether either of you had anything to do with these murders. The evidence that either of you were connected must be conclusive."

Lavinia sat in contemplation, her right thumb and forefinger clamped to the bridge of her nose. "I don't know, Davey. They have all that evidence. You have never even asked me if John and I did these things. Is that something we need to talk about? Do I need to tell you whether I indeed committed any murders?"

Heath shuffled his feet, obviously uncomfortable with the questions. He knew they had to talk about the murders. To put on a proper case, she had to be forthright with him. He did need to know what she and John would say at trial. How could there be any other explanations for the dead bodies found in the cellar and they not know about it? Then there would be Peeples' testimony. Yes, the defense would be tricky and for the most part, futile. "You don't have to come out with the words. I believe both of us know the facts in this case. I will have to be very creative in our defense. But trust me. In order to do so, we will need separate counsel for John."

"I will think about it. But whatever defense you put on, I will never sell out John."

"Understood," he responded.

On the twenty-fifth of February, the solicitor, James Caldwell, who would prosecute the case, was seen in an eating establishment with his friend, Chauncey Harriman, and overheard discussing the case, laughing and back-slapping. Although Heath was not quite the legal genius as were Caldwell and Harriman, upon learning of their improper association and collaboration on the matter, he was astute enough to file a grievance with the South Carolina State Court, asking that the two be investigated. This infuriated the men, prompting Harriman to summon Heath to his office the same day the state inquiry hit the magistrate's desk.

Harriman fired off the first volley. "What manner of nonsense is this, Mr. Heath?"

"Your honor, do you deny carrying on conversations with the solicitor about the case, openly receiving evidence from the man before my client's trial?"

Harriman sprang angrily to his feet. "How do you dare to level such charges on me? I will say one thing for you: you do have fight in you. And that I did not expect. You obviously have been getting advice from one of your moronic cohorts, because, Mr. Heath, you are not that intelligent! Who is advising you? Davenport? Hollingsworth?" He paused a moment, then sneered. "Oh, I see. Now it is quite apparent. This is something the bastard Cleary devised. Well, I will tell you one thing, you wet-nosed pip-squeak, between the both of you, there is as much knowledge on the law as a first year law student."

Heath stood his ground, folding his arms across his chest and balancing his weight determinedly between his firmly planted feet. "Don't bother asking Chief Cleary about this. I have not had so much as a word with him on the matter. But perhaps he *would* be interested in learning about such unethical and illegal behavior."

Leaning imposingly into Heath like a bully, out-weighing him two to one, the now ruddy- faced magistrate barked with spitting enunciation. "If you wish a fight with me, little man, I will give you one that you will never be able to win. I will tell you now to prepare your case by the second of April as the matter will be set on the docket for that day. I say that for I intend for these murderers to be in their graves by Easter. Rest assured, the good citizens of Charleston cannot wait to see these two are crucified. There will be no 'divine resurrection' this Easter. Quite the contrary, they'll be busy stoking Hell's furnace."

Refusing Harriman's intimidation, Heath took a half-step forward to place his face within inches of the judge. With taut lips and cemented jaw, he stared down his newly made foe and fired back. "What you have said here today I will use against you at the state convening...your honor. You have already convicted my clients in your mind and in doing so have tainted the inviolable office that you hold."

Harriman's bulbous eyes, noticeably scratched and reddened from Lavinia's nails, appeared poised to implode. With gritted teeth and clinched fists he retorted, "Leave this office at once or I will forget my position and smash you like the insignificant gnat that you are."

"As you have now threatened me, sir, this will likewise be a part of my report."

"*Get out!*" Harriman shouted, pointing to the door.

Davey Heath won but the first skirmish in his war with Chauncey Harriman. The upper court granted a stay until the charges against the magistrate could be addressed. The case would be postponed by the state indefinitely until some date to be determined, likely sometime in the spring.

Heyward was arraigned separately before Judge Bay as it was argued that the alleged conversation between Harriman and Caldwell did not include Heyward. No witness heard his name mentioned. Heyward's estranged wife, Elizabeth, posted the $100 bail, likely with money taken at the point of a gun from a traveler near Six Mile. He was released on the twenty-ninth. At Heyward's request, Davey Heath would represent him as well. He would be tried separately on the charges of robbery and murder.

The state attorney general arrived from Columbia on the thirtieth to review the complaint against Harriman, interviewing not only the subjects involved, but the citizens who were known to have witnessed the solicitor's and magistrate's conversation. After listening intently to Heath's passionate, persuasive argument, and interviewing both Harriman and Caldwell, he then took the witnesses' affidavits. To Heath's dismay, none of the citizens would admit they heard the dialogue between the two officials for fear of Harriman's retaliation. Now the attorney general would have no ammunition to use against them. At Heath's request, the state investigator interviewed Cleary regarding the attempted rape on Lavinia Fisher. The attorney general agreed that these were "serious and grievous charges indeed." Harriman vehemently disputed the charges, saying that he only "visited the wench out of curiosity," as she was a woman accused of massacring at least five men. And as there had never been a woman to his knowledge who had ever killed anyone in his jurisdiction, Harriman wanted to be sure the Chief had not concocted a bogus case against Lavinia Fisher. Unfortunately, the woman attacked him while interviewing her and he had the scars to prove it. Does the word of a magistrate judge not take preponderance over a mere constable?

The official findings were that there was insufficient information to make a propriety case against the magistrate or solicitor. However, the state further dictated that the Fisher case would be heard before a panel of judges with Judge Eliher Hall Bay presiding. A new trial attorney was appointed as well. It was the twenty-eight-year-old State Attorney General himself, Robert Y. Hayne. Much to the dismay of Cleary and Heath,

Harriman would also share the bench with the aging Judge Bay. The stay was lifted and the new trial date was May 27th. A subpoena was served on John Peeples in Albany, Georgia, to appear as a material witness. He would have to revisit his nightmare and face his would-be assailants one more time.

On Easter Sunday, Matthew Cowher returned to the Old Jail to visit Lavinia, bringing her warm pumpkin bread, toilet water and another blanket. The cell was cold and damp, especially at night, and she fought a persistent cough. She usually sat or slept wrapped from neck to feet in the moth-eaten wool blanket that had previously covered drunks and disease-ridden vagrants. It was like putting on a new body to have a clean, soft blanket that did not smell of beer, piss and body odor.

This time, Matthew was allowed to go inside the cell to minister to Lavinia. As soon as he closed the door, Cleary returned to his office. He was the only officer on duty, except for a young constable who had no family in the area, and was making his rounds through the much-deserted Charleston streets. He was to join the Clearys for Easter dinner later in the day.

It was noon and every church bell in the city rang out in praise on the day the world set aside to celebrate the Resurrection of the Messiah. Matthew sat on the edge of the cot beside Lavinia, head in hands, listening to the chimes and praying. Lavinia opened a fold in the blanket and placed her hand softly on Matthew's arm. "They're going to hang me, you know," she said. "The trial will just be a formality."

"Don't give up hope, Lavinia. You know you must pay for your crimes, but a woman has never been hanged in South Carolina, and I am not sure the civilized citizens of Charleston will allow it."

"Harriman and the others will decide my fate. He has surely already made up his mind, especially considering the embarrassment of his failed attack on me. And I don't believe the good citizens will go against the man as there are many who fear him."

Matthew turned his face to hers and nodded. "Whatever the case, you must be ready to face your judgment...that of man *and* God."

"I am not afraid to die, Matthew. And if there is a God, I am not afraid of Him either." She turned her face away and toward the outside wall. He noticed that even under her blanket she looked thin and pale. She had neither much to eat nor any sunlight these long weeks.

"Please don't blaspheme your God, Lavinia. Be assured He does exist, and He knows you better than any one of us. It is not too late to ask forgiveness and for your salvation. Heaven is not closed to you. The precious blood of Jesus Christ was shed for you as well as for me." Matthew's eyes were pained and his plea, earnest.

She shook her head, keeping it turned from him. They sat motionless and without word for a few moments, then she said almost in whisper "The only thing I need today is for you to hold me."

Matthew looked surprised, but as she fell tenderly into his chest, he put his arms around her. It wasn't anything sensual or sexual, but it was *loving*. They sat embraced for nearly a half-hour. At one point Matthew thought she had fallen asleep. It was obvious that she hadn't slept much from the cold, the stench, the roaches. Her beautiful eyes were tired and puffy, her face, drawn. He moved a little and she opened her eyes. "I must go," he said. "I have vespers at four."

As she stirred and opened her eyes, Lavinia began coughing again. "Matthew, would you do something for me?"

"If it is within my power. What do you need, my dear?"

"First, will you go to see my husband? I know nothing of his condition. Colonel Cleary told me he had been ill, having trouble keeping food on his stomach. If you could look in on him and give me a report, I would be much in your debt."

"It will be no bother. I will see to it directly."

"I have a second request," Lavinia continued. "Would you go to my house and bring to me my wedding dress. It has always been my favorite and I would like to wear it at my trial."

"At your trial?" Matthew was taken aback at this unusual request.

"Yes. Perhaps it will allow me to appear guiltless. White is the color of innocence and piety, you know." She managed a half-smile. This quippiness was good to hear, and Matthew thought he saw a little color restored in her face.

He still wore the confused expression. "I am not convinced of the value of this thing you ask, but I will do as you request."

As he stood up to leave, she stopped him with her touch on his hand. "You will not find the dress in any closet. It is hidden away in a false wall in my bedroom. If you will push on the wall between the fireplace and the west window, it will move. An opening will appear just wide enough for you to enter a small room. There you will find my gown and other valuables. As I have heard that robbers have made off with much of our possessions, I am sure there is no way they would have found this room."

Matthew nodded. "I will go there on the morrow," he said.

"Thank you." She took his hand and kissed it, then looked up at him from the bed, telling him with her eyes that she loved him. Given another time and another world, they would have been lovers. Perhaps still somewhere in time in some distant land where waters were pure and the valleys lush, she would live with him as his wife, even if it must be a minister's wife, and then, only then would she become a child of light.

On the morning of the 26th it was breezy and cold for an April day in Charleston, certainly cold enough for Matthew to throw a scarf around his neck and button down the wool coat tightly at the collar. As he guided his horse along the cobblestone streets, past the Old Jail and toward the Ashley Bridge, he could not help thinking of Lavinia in that loathsome cell, shivering, frightened, and so very lonely. It seemed like a nightmare, her being there, and her beauty wasting away along with her health. His brain conjured up an image of her serving the large basted bird two Christmases ago when she had him, the slave man Robert and his wife from the Alcott Plantation a mile down the road to dinner. Quincy Alcott who had also dined several times at Six Mile was a friend of Lavinia's parents, and he 'lent' Robert to her on occasion to help with the gardening. How could such a woman whose warm heart befriended ill-fated slaves take the lives of other human beings? White beings. It all made no sense. But the choices she made put her in that cell. Could he have said or done something more to save her? To help her open her heart to God?

As he approached the lane that led to the house, he noticed even at mid-morning how ghostly the place looked. A lazy fog still clung to the emerald meadow like cotton. The evergreen bushes and trumpet vines had been taken over by weeds and the house itself revealed the fractures and scars delivered at the hands of the vandals and robbers.

With the claw hammer he kept in his saddlebag to use in case he was assailed on the road by rogues, he began removing two boards nailed across the door to the walls on either side.

With the key Cleary gave him, he turned the lock and swung open the door. The robbers had indeed raped the house. There was a broken dining chair flung against a wall and the china closet had been overturned. The house smelled musty and a pungent odor reeked throughout, perhaps from spoiled food somewhere, or could it be the remnants of the decayed corpses in the basement. The thought of that made him shiver. And the thought of Lavinia sending five or more men to their deaths sickened him. The house was deafeningly quiet and he felt like he was standing in some man-made catacomb.

Matthew ascended the staircase, finding Lavinia's bedroom on the left. Her artistic touch was prevalent throughout the room. The thieves did not take the rose and Federal blue drapes, stitched by her own hand that cheerfully complemented the lavish, opulent silk wallpaper. Matthew correctly assumed the lifestyle and luxury to which she had become accustomed over the years could only have been acquired from the contents of her dead boarders' purses. The pittance the Fishers received for room and board would have otherwise barely allowed them to maintain a status quo. How long had she and John Fisher been in the business of murder?

Shaking off the mental picture of dead men dumped one onto another, he worked his way along the wall, pressing and pushing panels until one opened up into a small room scarcely bigger than a closet. A myriad of colorful dresses hung on a rack above what looked like a dozen pair of shoes Lavinia had ordered from Paris. There was a sewing basket, books of poetry by Robert Burns and Alexander Pope, and a portrait of a beautiful woman leaning against a wall.

Matthew picked up the painting and holding it out to his front with both hands, he knew immediately it was Lavinia. The artist had so profoundly captured the seduction and haunting beauty in her blue eyes. The half-smile had a noble but playful quality that could just as well have belonged to an Arabian princess or a Shakespearean Dock Street actress. He recognized the signature at the bottom right as that of Christopher Marshall, whom she obviously had commissioned to paint her, apparently some time within the past two or three years. But why had she not hung it in the parlor over the fireplace or in her bedroom? Did she not think it a good likeness?

Another larger book caught his eye. It appeared to be some kind of journal or diary, and when he opened it, shouting from the pages were years of passionate observations and encumbrances beginning in 1800, penned by an eight-year-old girl. Her soul, the very soul that she renounced and purged, lay wounded and bleeding somewhere in those words.

The last garment on the rack was the lovely white dress trimmed with lace jabots at the neck and wrists. Matthew wondered how she could have afforded the dress nearly a decade ago, especially considering she had just inherited little more than a struggling inn when her aunt died. He took down the dress and wrapped it in a sheet so that it would not soil from the sweat of his horse. He also found a piece of rope, tied off the painting and slung it over his shoulder. Shoving the diary into his coat, he descended the staircase into the parlor.

As his curiosity about the guestroom got the better of him, he walked along the creaky hallway, paused to take a breath at the door and entered the room. For the first time, the reality of the heinous crimes hit his mind. Men had died here at the hands of his young friend. Someone had taken the bed, perhaps the police or maybe a warped souvenir hunter. The hinged floor section was left hanging down into the cellar, exposing the large rectangular hole. Another deep breath, then Matthew peered into the hole. He really didn't expect to see anything down there as the bodies had been buried on the grounds. But suddenly there was movement. His heart jumped into his throat, causing him to stumble backward. "God!" he exclaimed. Taking a second cautious look, he saw that it was a large rat, probably searching for any decayed flesh that was not previously retrieved. This was enough for him and he quickly removed himself from the room to the front porch. More deep breaths.

After a while he closed and locked the front door, shutting out any further horror from the world. Slinging the dress and portrait over the pommel, he mounted the saddle and pointed his horse toward the road. At the end of the lane by the sign that read *Six Mile Inn*, he turned around in his saddle and took one final look back. He would never see the place again.

CHAPTER TEN

After taking Lavinia her dress, Matthew visited John Fisher as he promised, finding him no worse for wear and certainly not any sicker than he had found Lavinia. Fisher received Matthew coldly. The pangs of jealousy still inhabited the man, even though it really didn't matter anymore. The gallows would soon end all his emotions.

"I suppose you've been down there to see my wife, minister," John said, staring menacingly. "Been making regular visits, have you?"

"Today is only my third visit since her incarceration, Mr. Fisher. My heart finds it difficult to see her in such a state."

Fisher scowled. "I'm sure." He spat on the floor. "What is it about you, Parson? I've seen the way you make over her, look at her, read to her. You've wanted my Lavinia all the while we have been wed. You, a man of years and religion, doting over my young wife. It is not a natural thing, minister, and you violate your very oath."

"Mr. Fisher. You have no reason to think such a thing. I have known Lavinia since she was a child…a child in torment. I took her in as I would a daughter. But she would not stay in the church's care. I have only been interested in her welfare and the saving of her soul. If you insinuate I had any personal notions about her, you are gravely mistaken."

Moving closer to the cell door, Fisher's eyes remained fixed on Matthew's. "She does not even look at me the way she does you. She speaks of you as the perfect man and often measures me to you. How do you think that makes me feel?"

"I am sorry that you have these feelings, Fisher. But you must understand. I have loved her as I love all of God's creatures. Some need more attention than others. You must believe I have had no designs on Lavinia. If you do not believe that, then add that to your list of problems, sir." He turned to walk away.

Fisher watched Matthew's form fade into the dark corridor. "Minister!" he called.

Matthew came back into Fisher's view.

"How is she?"

"Cold. Pale. Undernourished."

Fisher dropped his head and didn't respond. Matthew edged closer to the bars and continued. "But otherwise, she seems well and asks about you."

"If you...when you see her again, give her my love."

Matthew's eyes softened, then he nodded and turned away.

The houses on Morrey Street were narrow across the front, usually no more than fifty feet across, but a hundred or more feet in depth. As homeowners were taxed by the city according to their frontage, these shotgun style houses were generally built to fit the elongated lots. A few of the houses on the street, however, breathed more comfortably as they were situated on larger lots, nestled under magnificent magnolias and rustic palmettos and bordered by stately wrought-iron or white picket fences. As these houses reflected the wealth and status of their occupants, taxable frontage was of little issue.

One such dwelling on Morrey belonged to Chauncey Harriman. Behind the white three-story were several outbuildings, including the kitchen house, a woodshed with a blacksmithy operation, a carriage house and the privy.

After a hefty plate of eggs, ham and grits, coupled with the noxiously shrill voice of his invalid wife calling "Chauncey.

Chauncey," Harriman's colon was ready to explode. Running down the stairs and out the back door, morning paper jammed into his armpit, he hit the privy seat just in time. With the tempest passed and his intestines fully purged, he peered through a crack in the privy wall at the shapely form on the other side. Kendra whisked back and forth from the kitchen to the house, toting dishes and pans, and singing some 'God-awful' spiritual.

Kendra was a happy sort, good-natured and full of life in spite of her bondage. She knew she did not have it as bad as other slave women. She had heard horror stories of women working in the rice fields, some cut to ribbons by their master's whip, and others keeling over from sunstroke upon the very earth where they toiled. Mistress Harriman treated her well and even Harriman himself was not all that bad to her, except when bellowing for his dinner or berating her if she dropped a dish.

With his pants below his fat calves, Harriman sat long after his privy business watching Kendra with a lecherous eye. She stopped not ten feet from the outhouse to pull a clump of weeds away from the much over-grown chard vine that clung to a fence post. She bent over, unwittingly advertising her plump buttocks to him under her unseasonable tulle gingham dress. And Chauncey was in the market. Fully done now with his morning constitutional, he pushed open the door, startling Kendra.

"Master Chauncey!" she exclaimed, holding a hand over her breasts. "I didn't know you were there."

"My but don't you look pretty today, Kendra," Harriman said, buttoning his trousers while taking inventory of the body under that gingham.

"Thank you, suh. Nice of you to say so." She then turned away to walk back toward the house, her warm, sweet vapor spilling into the frosty air as she tottered off.

Harriman quickly caught up to her and stroked the right cheek of her buttocks with a large hand. She tensed up and kept walking, but without protest. She knew she couldn't or she may find herself sold away from her family to some butcher and laboring as a field hand.

A voice from behind them suddenly boomed in their direction, causing Harriman to flinch. "Misres Harriman is calling for you, Master Chauncey." Marcus, standing by the tool shed like a Zulu warrior, hammer embedded in a clenched fist, bit his lip to keep from saying more. The fierce eyes reflected his hatred for the man, but he knew there would be a risk in taking the matter to the next level. Mrs. Harriman was remarkably not calling this time, but Marcus had to say something to get Harriman's filthy hand off Kendra.

"Marcus, you ignorant savage, get back to work! That horse will not shoe himself."

To defuse what could be a painful end to this conversation, Kendra spoke up. "I will run up to see what Misres Harriman needs."

Marcus turned without further word and went back to work at the anvil. Soon the hammer began to clang again, shaping one horseshoe after another under the red-hot flame. If only it were his master's head at the end of that hammer.

"Are you awake?" The woman's voice roused Lavinia from her state of semi-consciousness. She was still not sleeping well, but then there were moments when she was deeply under, only to be sharply awakened by the scratching of a rat in the wall or the raspy cough of a drunken prisoner down the corridor.

Gathering her senses, Lavinia raised her body to a sitting position on the bed, finding Margaret Cleary peering through the bars. Margaret was as usual stern-faced, but today there was a kindly glow about her that almost gave Lavinia a feeling of kinship to the woman. The face was a welcomed refuge from the days of suffocating blackness that had taken toll on Lavinia's sanity. She had been left to consider herself worth little more than the vermin that abode with her in the cell.

"Mrs. Cleary. Why are you...is there something you want?" The words choked out of her mouth, lacking coherency. Perhaps because she had been out of practice communicating with other human beings except telling a constable to "no, take it away" when he brought the day's swill.

"You may call me Margaret if you wish, Lavinia. Mind you, this does not indicate in any way a friendship, as I certainly remained abhorred at your grievous acts of murder."

Lavinia dropped her eyes, indicating something between embarrassment and shame. "I understand," she replied.

"In speaking with my husband, I find he has been quite concerned about your wellness, specifically your color and complexion. I too see that you appear pale and undernourished. I have taken upon myself to bring you some beef roast and carrots, and this jar of cream to erase the roughness from your skin.

"Mrs. Cleary...Margaret. I care not what I look like. I am soon to die anyway, so what does it matter if my skin resembles that of a lizard?"

"I see the dress hanging yonder that you asked the Reverend bring you to wear at your trial. I should think that if you intended to look your best in it, you would be concerned of her appearance otherwise."

Lavinia stood wobbly to her feet. "What I would rather have is the pistol you so aptly stuck in that pig, the magistrate's ear, so I could end my life quickly and cheat the city from its day of execution."

"I have no doubt of your guilt, Lavinia, but when justice is done, you could very well be spared the rope and instead spend the remainder of your years in a cell such as this."

"All the more reason to end my life now. I would never survive as a prison rat. If you really cared about something as trivial as my appearance, then care enough to bring me the gun."

"You know I cannot do that," Margaret replied. "And will not. I will only tend to your needs and make you as comfortable as possible these next few weeks." She paused and scanned Lavinia, head to toe. "It is still beyond my ability to understand why a woman such as you could do what you did. Help me understand, Lavinia."

"Don't concern yourself with it, Margaret. You wouldn't understand anyway," Lavinia said tartly.

"Try me."

"Do you really want to know or are you just curious, anxious to take the story of the lowly murderess, Lavinia Fisher, to the *Charleston Free Press* or to the bitches of the Marlborough Street Society Club?"

Margaret squinted and drew her mouth into a scowl. "Whether you believe my sincerity or not, I am not here to gather gossip fodder. I am here to see to the sanitary needs of a woman prisoner. I…..just thought you'd like to have the ear of another woman, that's all. If my questions offend you, then so be it. I won't trouble you further." She turned into the darkness to leave.

"Wait," Lavinia said softly. "Please pull the chair up to the door."

Margaret picked up the mold-coated chair, placed it near the cell, and spread her handkerchief over the seat before gracefully sitting down.

Lavinia sat down on the edge of her bed as well. "You are fortunate to have had a man like Colonel Cleary. I bear him no ill will for arresting me. He was doing his job, but then knowing what I did, he has still treated me with the same respect he would give any woman of greater culture and refinement than me."

"He is a fine husband as well and I thank you for your words. But we are talking about you. I am certainly aware you have had no friends in this city...nary a woman with whom you could confide." She stopped and quipped, "Of course, the heinous deeds you committed, you would have kept to yourself, anyway. But I do now realize the scorn you have suffered, largely for not fitting in with the social crowd. Since your arrest I have heard the tongues wag, and unfortunately have learned about you through them. But I myself have avoided many of these women who feed off the table of sophistication and pretentiousness. They are just not my cup of tea." Margaret immediately felt ill at ease about her tea metaphor, as it was indeed her cups of tea that put Lavinia behind that cell door in the first place.

Lavinia settled deeper into the cot and placed her back against the wall. She brushed floor dirt from the hem of the dress that she had worn day after day.

"It was all about the money, you know. At first it was, anyway. But then there were other reasons. Somewhere along the way I developed a disdain for fat men with fat purses. Strutting around Six Mile like the pompous pigs they were, they stuffed their jaws with my food, swilled my ale, and bragged about their business deals, flaunting their importance like we were nobodies." Lavinia then grit her teeth and balled up her fists. "But we showed them, Margaret. We showed them who had the real power——the power to control life and death. We took their miserable lives and did it with style." She tossed her black head of hair and lifted her chin as if it were a defiant amen.

Margaret appeared stunned. The normally determined eyes transformed into doe eyes. Although she knew any dialogue about murder would be uncomfortable to carry on, she didn't expect Lavinia to be so boastful of her crimes. "But these men chose your house as a rest haven to their busy lives. They trusted you and paid you their money for food and lodging, and you then took the men from their families…and without a sense of remorse."

"Perhaps it was their destiny to die, Margaret. Just as surely as it was their destiny to choose staying at Six Mile House."

Margaret scooted her chair back a little and grasped a cell bar to stand. "You had no right to play God and executioner, Lavinia. You punished these men because they were wealthy and enjoyed stature. You do deserve to die, you know."

Lavinia stood and moved to the bars, placing her hand delicately onto Margaret's. "I know," she said softly, smiling. "And that is *my* destiny."

Margaret withdrew her hand quickly as though she had been touched by evil itself. "I will say a prayer for you, my dear. Keep the jar of cream and dress your skin. You will need to restore your radiance to help your defense."

"Goodbye, Margaret." She paused and smiled again. "Thanks. You're a kind woman. I am sure if things had been different we could have been friends. You're not like the others in this town."

Margaret reflected a moment and nodded. "You know the word 'goodbye' is actually the shortened English bid, 'God Be With Ye.' And may He be indeed. Now I must check on Nate. He will be looking for his dinner."

The moon low over the Atlantic cast a long, silver ribbon of light across the waters and into the sea battery. Each glistening night wave danced with rhythmic timing, breaking softly against moss-covered rocks and barnacle-crusted pilings. The night air was brisk for this twenty-sixth of May. According to the Almanac, 1819 South Carolina was to experience a less than mild spring and this cool night under the annealed stars and vibrant moon certainly gave credence to the prediction.

Matthew's solace was interrupted by the clop clopping of hooves on the ballast stone. The rider was at first a mere form, faceless and vague, camouflaged by the night, but soon a familiar image, the impeccably-dressed Nathaniel Cleary, materialized in the velvet rays of the climbing moon.

"It is a beautiful night, eh, Matthew?"

"Splendid, my friend. Should you not be enjoying such an evening at home with Margaret? "

"Indeed. But as tomorrow will be a day of immense importance in this city, I am tonight sharing rounds with my officers. We will all need to be at our best as I suspect there will be a veritable army of Charlestonians lining the streets when the prisoners are paraded to the courthouse."

Matthew turned his face to the moon and re-lit his pipe. The sudden pungent aroma of the burly tobacco mercifully shut out the indignant stench of slain mackerel from the fish house adjacent to the dock.

Cleary dismounted and joined the minister with a cigar, both leaning against the pilings. "I dread what will happen tomorrow. Harriman will make quick work of the matter and if he has his way, the woman and her conspirators will be hanging from the rope by day's end."

Matthew allowed the hot bowl of his pipe to warm his hands, then shoved them into his pockets. He didn't immediately respond, but then through the teeth that clenched his pipe said, "I remember the little girl's face as vividly this night as when I first saw it some twenty years ago. Sweet. Scared. Innocent. When the church took her in, I desperately tried helping her fend off the demon voices that haunted her soul. She would not speak for weeks after the massacre and when I looked in on her at night, finding her fretful and tormented by her dreams, shaking and weeping, my own words did little to comfort her. I am convinced, Nathaniel, that the horror of the blood-letting on that day caused that little girl to lose all faith in what is good and right, propelling her into a life of madness."

"I suspect you are right, Matthew. And I do not take issue with you on that; however, she chose to take up a destructive path and whatever the catalyst, good men lie in their graves. The law will neither consider nor sanctify her infirmities, but will instead consider her as either possessed by Satan himself or as black-hearted as any other cold and calculating killer. Perhaps your conversation should be with Mr. Heath. He will certainly need any such ammunition if this woman is to be saved. As it is scarcely seven-thirty, I am sure he is burning the lamp oil to-night to prepare himself for the case."

"Thank you, Nathaniel. Perhaps you are right. I will visit him. I have been reading some material that recently fell into my hands that may help her case as well."

The men shook hands and departed the dock, leaving only the sound of lapping waters and the returning odor of decaying fish.

CHAPTER ELEVEN

May 27th, 1819

A crowded squalor of curious onlookers, staid merchants, society matrons, vagrants and slaves alike poured into the street outside of the courthouse. This would be the most significant trial of the young century, perhaps within the previous fifty years. This trial would decide the fate of a woman. And that woman could be the first to be hanged in the State of South Carolina.

A select number of citizens were given the privilege of observing the proceedings and were allowed to enter the courtroom at eighty-thirty. Others swarmed onto the grounds, climbing walls and trees to gain advantage in hopes of seeing the woman through the window. The remainder huddled in a mass of hundreds, some standing on sullied soil, contaminated by wastewater, horse manure and piss.

Chauncey Harriman arrived around eight-forty five in his carriage driven by Marcus. The magistrate looked much like an English baron in his top hat, gray jacket with tails and a new wig that better complemented his pompous face. To further flaunt his affluence, Harriman had even outfitted Marcus with a jacket and wide-brimmed hat to declare his slave as 'best in show.' After dismounting from his carriage, the big man pushed out his arms to the crowd to acknowledge the phony cheers, tipping his hat several times to the more attractive ladies who lined the steps of the courthouse.

The next to arrive was Judge Bay. Although there was not as much heraldry as with Harriman, there was indeed an air of grandiose self-importance as he was accompanied by a flock of associates carrying law books and valises, each speaking to no one.

Robert Hayne, assuming the role of solicitor in the trial, and who had just enjoyed a fine breakfast at the home of an associate, Jeremy Scott, walked with his friend along Broad to the courthouse once described by novelist William Simms as "big, solid, square and lofty." Hayne, strikingly handsome in appearance and presence with expressionless gray eyes, was a superb orator. Ten years later he would be Daniel Webster's opponent in the "Great Debate of 1830." Hayne, a true advocate of states' rights, formulated the position of "tariff for revenue only."

Pushing his way through the crowd in the street then came Davey Heath, mostly unnoticed and without the pageantry. One or two citizens shouted, "There's the lawyer!" or "You haven't got a chance in hell gettin' them off, Heath. They's good as hanged."

The buzz of the mob was suddenly reduced to a hush as a path was cleared for Chief Constable Cleary, three of his officers and two prisoners shackled together, a man and a woman. The silence then turned to jeers and shouts, mostly from men of all character and class, and a few brash women of questionable repute. The women of society put their heads together, pointing at the woman in the wedding dress, hands shackled at her slim waist and head down. From the time Lavinia entered the crowd until she climbed the steps to the courthouse, she made no eye contact with anyone. By the time she was seated in the courtroom, she noticed that her beautiful white dress had collected a dozen or so splotches from the mud balls and tomatoes tossed in her direction.

The trial attracted the attention of the press as far south as St. Augustine and to the north, Philadelphia, mostly due to the fact that William Hastings was one of the latter city's victims. Mainly, there was immense interest in the woman known as Lavinia who may have been the young country's first mass murderess and the first woman to be hanged in America since the country gained its independence from English rule. As many a woman had been hanged or trephined in Seventeenth Century Massachusetts, accused of witchcraft or demonic possession, Lavinia Fisher would face the gallows in South Carolina for the most heinous of crimes against humanity, historically always committed by men.

The atmosphere of the courtroom was 'chill and electric with excitement' as the *Free Press* captured it. Though the capacity of the courtroom was no more than fifty people, five times that many had congregated in the hallway and on the outer steps and another two hundred along Broad Street. At the solicitor's table sat Hayne and several associates, already peering over legal documents and notes. Heath sat at the adjacent table in thoughtful pose with eyes closed, stroking his forehead. To his right, Lavinia and John Fisher held shackled hands and whispered to each other. It was the first day in five months they had seen one another. John took note that she was perhaps fifteen pounds lighter, looking tired and wanly. But with the aid of Margaret Cleary, Lavinia's hair and face were done in such impeccable detail that with the exception of the street-smudged gown, one may instead picture her occupying a church pew or banquet table.

John Fisher did choose the services of another lawyer, an associate of Heath, Jeffrey Withrow. He sat on Fisher's left. Would Fisher be given up in an effort to save Lavinia's life? The only course for Withrow would be an appeal for mercy.

Behind the solicitor's table were Colonel Cleary and Margaret, Constable Miller and John Peeples. In the end seat just behind Heath, Matthew Cowher prayed, head bowed, eyes closed, hands folded and tips of his fingers on the bridge of his nose. When he had finished, he slowly lifted his head to find Lavinia's eyes on him. The eyes were sad, fearful and unblinking. After a few moments she turned back toward the bench where Chauncey Harriman, her would-be rapist, and Judge Bay would this day pass sentence on her.

At nine-thirty the bailiff stood and shouted, "Hear ye, hear ye! The court of the Honorable Judge Elihu Hall Bay of the District Court of Charleston County is now in session. God save the United States of America and the glorious State of South Carolina, in the year of our Lord, eighteen hundred nineteen. All rise!"

Judge Bay first took his position behind the bench. Then while the assembly of officials, the accused and observers were still standing, Harriman in a black robe, creating a grand image likened only to the Messiah at the Second Coming, swept through the rear door and ascended onto his chair at the bench.

Judge Bay, old and nearly deaf, had the reputation for making unorthodox rulings. Although well revered, he often injected a bit of humor into the courtroom, sometimes in his rulings. He once sentenced two revelers who had gotten into a fight and charged with 'biting' to share the same cell for two days so they could "bite each other until there were no remains left." However, on this important day, given his deafness and ill health, he yielded a portion of the judicial administration to Judge Harriman.

Rapping his gavel sharply to quieten the courtroom, the presiding Judge Bay began his profound soliloquy, allowing his ego-resounding voice to resonate throughout the room and down the hallway.

"We gather here this glorious May day of eighteen and nineteen to consider the fate of those accused, standing here before this jury of noble men, to determine their innocence or guilt of the terrible crimes committed against the poor souls taken from this world before their natural time. Master Heath! To the charges of murder in the first degree, what says the accused?"

Heath looked at Lavinia then back to the judge. "Your honor, Lavinia Fisher pleads not guilty."

An unintelligible murmur permeated from the gallery and the judge rapped the gavel again, three times. Normally unperturbed and impartial, Bay cast a look of scorn and displeasure over his glasses and into the faces of the defendants.

"And to you, Mr. Withrow, what says the accused?"

Without hesitating, he replied, "Not guilty."

"And to the charges of armed robbery perpetrated on numerous occasions upon wayfarers and Charleston citizens alike, what say you both?"

"Not guilty," stated both Heath and Withrow.

Bay struck his gavel again and paused to render each defendant a disapproving stare. "You may take your seats. Proceed with the county's case, Mr. Hayne. I will ask that everyone speak up, for as you all know the Good Lord has left me in my old age with the ability to hear from only one ear. And I don't hear so well from that one." Then he laughed, giving latitude for others in the court to respectfully echo their chuckles as well.

The solicitor gathered himself slowly to his feet so as to be dramatic and in eloquent tongue, he began:

"My dear gentlemen of the jury. You see before you two vicious and calculating criminals who committed unspeakable acts against humanity and who with pre-meditation and a devaluation of human life, slaughtered an unknown number of men, then disposing of their remains in the cellar. This took place at the accused Fisher residence, a place known as Six Mile House. We will provide indisputable evidence of these crimes through the testimony of an eyewitness, seated there, who himself was a would-be victim, but miraculously escaped, putting an end to their reign of terror. Our most respected physician there (gesturing toward Dr. Stevens, seated beside Cleary), will attest to finding five decomposing sets of remains beneath the flooring of the inn operated by John and Lavinia Fisher. The county intends to prove as well that the Fishers organized and commanded a vicious gang of highwaymen who preyed upon merchants and wayfarers in the territory north of this city, robbing, assaulting and murdering scores, terrorizing this entire community for God only knows how many years." The words, as always, were delivered with fluency and precision.

As Hayne continued his oratory, describing the events and findings at Six Mile in gruesome detail, several of the women in the courtroom gasped and placed handkerchiefs over their mouths. One fell limp in her chair and Dr. Stevens administered smelling salts. Realizing that his account of the murders at the inn might be perhaps too graphic and construed as over-kill, Solicitor Hayne then presented the armed robbery case. In succinct detail he told of the secured masks and stolen property found in the house, the barn and an out building. He paced back and forth along the row of jurors, hands behind him, sometimes stopping to place them on the railing for effect to drive home his points.

Hayne would not belabor the robberies, however. Although men had been hanged for less, a woman would not swing from a rope for robbery alone. His case would be about murder. The highway robberies would be the icing on his well-baked cake if the matter went as well as he hoped. When he had completed his final statement, he glared at the defendants, then bowed before the judges. Bay nodded as though to say "well done", then turned his head to Heath. "Your opening, counselor."

Heath glanced at his client and stood, placing his fingertips on the table. "Your honor, I will waive my opening statement and instead reserve my comments as to my client's innocence for my closing summation."

Harriman spoke up to register his annoyance. "Mr. Heath. That is most unusual for a trial of this magnitude. I suggest that you are doing a disservice to your client's defense. Do you intend to make the solicitor's job this easy?"

"Not at all, sir. I have already simply stated the defense's position by pleading her absence of guilt."

"Very well, counselor," replied Harriman. "As you have been prone to courtroom errors in the past, I fear I am compelled to watch after you, so that you do not facilitate in the hanging of your own client."

"Yes, your honor."

"Mr. Withrow," Harriman continued. "Your opening."

"Your honors, we wish to waive any opening remarks as well."

The magistrate continued staring down both lawyers as Judge Bay cleared his throat. "Master Hayne. You may call your first witness."

The solicitor stood in response. "The County of Charleston calls John Peeples."

Peeples rose from his chair and eyed the accused with fear and caution as he made his way to the box. He repeated the oath and took his place at the witness stand. Hayne then asked Peeples to lay out the events of the day he arrived at Six Mile House. Peeples appeared nervous at first, stuttering as he gave his account. Occasionally, he glanced in Lavinia's direction, but avoided any lengthy eye contact. As he unfolded the events, the court listened intently without uttering even a whisper. He told of the gracious way he was received and fed, and of the offer of tea, which he refused. He told of the two men outside of the guestroom window plotting his death and then materializing in his room to fire a mini-ball into what they believed was his sleeping body. Peeples stopped abruptly, as horror revisited his face. He asked for a cup of water, drank it and continued. He told of Lavinia's appearance and her anger about losing her precious quilt. The gallery murmured and Bay rapped once with his gavel, which sounded like the sharp report of a pistol. Everyone in the courtroom jumped in startled reflex.

"That's all I have to say," said Peeples. He was instructed to remain seated for cross-examination.

"I have no questions for the witness, your honor."

"Mister Heath!" bellowed Harriman. "I have warned you that it is your responsibility to provide a proper defense for your client, and you appear to be reticent if not reckless in the discharge of your duties." Judge Bay looked toward Harriman, somewhat amazed, even annoyed with his berating of Heath.

"No questions, your honor."

Harriman shook his head and shot a puzzled look in the direction of Hayne, sarcastically throwing up his hands. "And I suppose you do not wish to question the witness as well, Mr. Withrow?"

Withrow stood and nodded. "That is correct, your honor."

Harriman turned to Judge Bay and cast a look of bewilderment.

Matthew appeared uneasy as well and repositioned himself in his chair. Lavinia was not fazed by Peeples' account or by the tensive dialogue between the court officers. Her emotionless eyes remained fixed on the table before her.

"I call Dr. Jervis Stevens," said Hayne.

The coroner reported his grim findings to the court, specifically examining the still recognizable remains of William Hastings, identified by a contract with the Farthmore Carriage Company in his pocket. Dr. Stevens had personally laid out the bones of four others that could not be identified. He shook his head as he gave his vivid and succinct description.

Again there was no cross-examination by Heath. Harriman dropped his head and rubbed his eyes.

"Then the prosecution rests, your honors," said Hayne.

Judge Bay struck the gavel again. "The court will be in recess until the fourteenth hour."

As the gallery's buzz ensued, people began to leave the courtroom in twos and threes. The prisoners were taken to a locked room and a constable posted at the door.

Davey Heath rose slowly and gathered up his documents. Matthew intercepted him before he could leave. "Mr. Heath. A moment, please." Heath turned and locked eyes on the minister.

"Yes, Reverend."

"In view of our conversation last evening, I want to give you this." Matthew pulled from inside his vest Lavinia's diary. "I will ask you to review it during the recess. Give your special attention to the fifth and twenty second pages."

"Is this the diary we discussed?"

"It is," replied Matthew.

"What value will it be to her case?"

Matthew laid the book in Heath's hands. "It will become apparent as you read through it, Davey. Now put on your case." Matthew grasped Heath by the shoulders and gave him a determined, five-second look. Heath then turned around, took an apple from his coat and sat back in his chair. There would be no lunch today at the Carter House. He would instead feast on the fruit and on Lavinia's journal.

Promptly at two, the command to rise was again given to the court. Hayne rested his case and Heath advised Harriman he was poised to present his clients' defense.

"It is nigh time, counselor," chided the magistrate.

"I call William Heyward to the stand."

Heyward stood, then walked in cowered posture to the witness chair. After being sworn in, he sat down.

"Mr. Heyward, how did you come to know the Fishers?"

Heyward glanced quickly at John Fisher. "John there did some work with me down at the city dock a few years back and we got to be mates. I'd come by the inn to catch one of Lavinia's meals, especially when she was havin' pork and beans and corn on the cob. I also played poker with John and some of their guests ever so often. Don't mind tellin' you I drank a little Scotch along with it."

Heath walked toward Heyward and placed his hand on the banister. "The man who told his story this morning, John Peeples. Have you ever seen him before?"

Heyward looked in Peeples' direction. "Yeah, I saw him there at Six Mile some time ago. We had dinner and then I left. I never said more'n two words to him."

"Why would he say he saw you enter his room with my clients and fire a pistol at his bed?"

"No idea. He said this mornin' it was dark in his room and if he saw someone, it weren't me and it weren't John and Lavinia, neither."

"Then you're telling the court the Fishers did not conspire with you to kill Mr. Peeples," Heath rephrased.

"That's exactly what I'm sayin.' And as far as the Fishers go, I've never known them to be anything but good and gracious to all their boarders and, furthermore, never knew them to raise a hand against another. I tell you, Mr. Heath, we weren't in that man's room and definitely never fired a gun at him or at a pillow."

Heath looked at the jurors, then at Peeples who was shaking his head. "I have no further questions for the witness."

It was Withrow's turn. He asked Heyward a couple of similar questions, receiving answers that very much mirrored his previous testimony. Both lawyers for the defense rested.

"Mr. Hayne, your witness," said Harriman.

Hayne stood and with hands on hips, staring menacingly into Heyward's face, walked pompously in his direction. Even though it appeared from his demeanor that he would pounce on Heyward like a bobcat on a rabbit, Hayne had a polite, even conciliatory way about him, direct but never browbeating. "Mister Heyward. How is it that this man, John Peeples, has singled you out, giving in such explicit detail the conversation you had with Fisher, the murderous plot you schemed, and your firing of the pistol at his bed? What motive would he have to drag you into this?"

Heath stood with an objection. "Your honors, this man is not being tried today. As he is also my client, he will soon have his own day in court. I would think this line of questioning would certainly prejudice, even serve to incriminate him."

Before the bench could address the objection, Hayne retorted. "This man is a material witness today for the state, your honors. He will merely convey what he knows about that evening, specifically as regards his friends, the accused. His testimony need not incriminate him, unless he wishes to come clean with the truth.

"Again, your honors, the defense objects."

Judge Bay, as usual colorless in complexion and expression, responded. "I must overrule the objection, counselor. You chose to put the man on the stand as a defense witness and therefore opened the door. Indeed, Mr. Peeples has conveyed a version of the incident which puts Mr. Heyward in the room with the accused. Any admission of co-conspiracy by Mr. Heyward would certainly prejudice his own case, but this man denies involvement, does he not?"

Heath stood with folded arms, digesting the ruling, gave a quick nod and wince, then sat down.

Hayne restated the question. "Mr. Heyward. Again, you heard Mr. Peeples' account of the evening that put you and the accused in the same room, conspiring to kill him. What say you about this?"

Heyward shook his head and looked down. "All I can say is I think he made the whole thing up."

"No, Mr. Heyward. I submit that it is you who are making up this story. Mr. Peeples has no reason to lie. He would rather be back in Georgia with his wife and four children than here putting an innocent man on the gallows."

"I again object, your honor," said Heath from his table. "Mr. Hayne has summarized to the jury that my client is guilty, and Mr. Heyward as well, before all evidence has been presented. Is he not manipulating the court with such statements?"

Bay neither sustained nor overruled the objection. "Do you have other questions for the witness, Mr. Hayne?"

"No, your honor. I believe the court has heard enough lies from this man."

As Heath shook his head again, Bay asked if he would prefer to readdress. Heath felt he needed to leave well enough alone and protect Heyward from further examination.

"Step down, Heyward," Harriman commanded. "Mr. Hayne, please proceed with the county's case."

"The county rests at this time, your honor."

Harriman nodded. "Then Mr. Heath and Mr. Withrow, continue."

It was Withrow who stood and motioned the officer to unlock Fisher's irons. "I call to the stand my client, John Fisher."

Asking the same round of questions, Withrow also probed the issue of the bodies beneath the house, especially that of William Hastings. He knew it would come up in Hayne's cross-examination, so he decided to lay out Fisher's account and take the offense. Fisher promised the court that he did not know how the bodies could have been dumped under the house. He supposed the man or men who killed these people were some of the same highwaymen who had been working the roads and had disposed of the bodies by way of the cellar door at the rear of the house. Neither he nor Lavinia had been in the cellar for years as it had flooded and pretty much stayed muddy.

Withrow then rested. Harriman asked Heath if he had questions for Fisher. Heath replied that he did not. He knew what questions were coming from Hayne and chose to reserve his right for cross-examination, especially if there was something said to incriminate his client.

Hayne stood, shook his head and grinned. "Your story, Mr. Fisher, has more holes than the chunk of Swiss cheese I had for lunch. I think I can sew up your pack of manufactured lies with these questions." He walked to the witness stand and put one hand on the magistrate's bench. "How is it the police found these bodies directly below the bed in the guests' room, the bed that would drop downward with the pull of a lever? And is not it incredible that Mr. Peeples would ever have known about the trap door unless he witnessed your failed attempt to send him to his grave? It is his account of the dropping bed that led the police to your very door. Furthermore, the police had to break into that cellar door and will attest that it had not been opened in years."

Fisher responded only with his eyes. He looked helplessly in the direction of his attorney, then Lavinia, but remained silent.

"Answer the question!" bellowed Harriman.

"He cannot, your honor," said Hayne. "The only answer is that he conspired with the two sitting there to murder their boarders and dispose of the remains in a place they hoped no one would ever look."

Withrow rose. "Objection, your honor. The solicitor answers for my client with suppositions and conjectures."

Hayne quickly responded. "Your honor, the man's silence alone convicts him. Apparently, he has nothing more to say. And as a matter of fact, neither do I. I will be anxious to hear the woman's story." He gave the jurymen a wink and chuckled as he walked back to his chair.

Fisher stood down and was re-shackled. Heath sat for a few moments with hands folded at his chin. There was an eerie stillness and anticipation in the courtroom awaiting Heath's calling of the woman. He knew neither Fisher nor Heyward would be credible nor were they thick-skinned enough to withstand Hayne's bombardment. Fisher was indeed as good as hanged, and his attorney could do nothing about it. If Fisher had hanged himself, as it was apparent that he did, then he was to become a throwaway pawn to set the stage for the only possible defense that could save Lavinia Fisher from hanging.

All eyes were on the woman that the gallery had come to hear. When summoned, Lavinia rose with as much dignity as a woman wearing a wedding dress to her trial could garner. She moved to the witness box and placed her hand on the Bible. This prompted her to give Matthew a smirky smile. She might as well have had her hand on a dictionary. But she did manage to repeat the phrase "so help me God."

Heath knew the prosecutor had as evidence her poison, the same poison extracted by Dr. Stevens from William Hastings' stomach. As this would be hard to overcome along with Peeples' testimony and the trap door evidence, Heath's questioning strategy to Lavinia would be different. He begged the court's pardon then bent over the railing to confer a few moments with Lavinia. She nodded a couple of times, shook her head emphatically *no* once, then shrugged her shoulders in resignation.

Heath stood silently at the stand for a few moments and then shocked the courtroom. "Mrs. Fisher, why did you kill those men?"

Hayne's jaw dropped at the same time the gallery exploded in fifty tongues. The gavel rapped again five or six times and Bay shouted, "I will have order in my courtroom! Counselor Heath! What manner of defense is this? Earlier you pled this woman *not guilty*. Have you now given up your client?"

Heath ignored the judge and drew closer to his client. "Please answer the question, Lavinia." Matthew leaned forward in his chair and interlocked his fingers. Bay looked at Harriman and threw up his hands in animated exhaustion.

Lavinia, who had been looking down the entire time, raised her eyes to her attorney's. "For the money, of course, Mr. Heath." John Fisher placed his hands over his face. Matthew sat emotionless, concentrating on Lavinia's face. Lavinia herself displayed a look of entitlement as though she had been justified in killing them. "They would not have given it up otherwise." There was again mumbling and glances of disbelief throughout.

Harriman leaned over the bench onto one elbow. "Counselor, I am not sure what your tactic is, but if you wish to change this woman's plea, we will dispense with the remainder of the trial and move on to the punishment stage."

"Your honor, my client does not intend to change her plea. Instead, I will show where her admission to the crimes will paradoxically support her *not guilty* plea."

"You are indeed the worst lawyer who has set foot in any courtroom. But, let's hear your nonsense to see if you will continue making a fool of yourself. After this fiasco, you may as well lock the door to your practice. You will not have so much as a vagrant seeking your services."

Again Heath ignored Harriman and drew from inside his coat the journal. After opening the book, he wet his thumb with his tongue and turned to the fifth page. "Lavinia, please read this page."

She burned holes in Matthew's eyes with hers. She knew only *he* could have found the diary in the room behind the false wall. "I will not, Mr. Heath."

"Then I will. Gentlemen of the jury, an eight-year-old girl wrote this nearly twenty years ago." He put on his spectacles and began:

"….the savages took everything from me when they killed my parents and brother. Why didn't they kill me, too? I am now dead inside anyway. There is no way I want to go on living…."

Hayne stood and interrupted, gesturing with an outstretched hand in Heath's direction. "Your honor, what relevance is this to the case. We are not at the Dock Street Theatre and this is not a play, though it appears counsel is making it one."

Heath looked over his glasses at both Bay and Harriman and said, "Give me latitude here, your honor. I will reveal to the court the importance of this journal."

Bay shrugged his shoulders in his usual crotchety manner and shook his head. "As it appears all the rules of courtroom decorum have fallen away, what does it further matter? Get on with it."

Lavinia gritted her teeth and squinted her eyes at Heath. "I do not wish for you to continue with this reading, sir."

Heath leaned into her and whispered. "Lavinia. I am sorry. The court must hear this. Please understand that this is your *defense* here."

She folded her arms and turned her head to the side to register contempt. But she did not further protest.

"I will continue on page twenty-two:

"*...it is my sixteenth birthday. No one has taken notice. And I have no friends who would be here. Auntie will not allow it. She keeps me locked in my room when there are boarders. She claims to be a Christian woman, but I know she has no love in her heart for me. What little my parents left me she has sold. Even my mother's jewelry, except the beautiful cameo that I have hidden. When Auntie found that it was missing, she accused me of stealing it and beat me with her large wooden spoon. The woman hates me. I have no love left in my heart for anyone. Except Matthew....*"

All heads in the courtroom turned to Matthew. Feeling their stares, he looked left and right, then returned his eyes to Lavinia. John Fisher scooted down in his chair and folded his arms in contempt. Heath continued reading..."*I cannot live on like this. I have nothing. I am nothing.*"

"Shall I go on, Lavinia? You wrote this." Heath then turned to the jury. "Gentlemen, this came from the mind of a very disturbed young girl who has had more than her share of grief and torment. She was made into what the prosecutor would consider a monster through no fault of her own."

Hayne stood again and objected. "Is this my esteemed colleague's summation or is this some type of devised trickery to make us believe she was not responsible for her murderous acts? Sounds to me this was nothing more than a sad young woman who felt the world had dealt her a bad hand. Many of us are handed such troubles and defeats, but does this give us license to take the lives and property of the innocent? Moreover, how can Mr. Heath continue to plead her not guilty when she admits she killed the lot?"

Harriman puffed himself up like a toad and let out a lengthy sigh. "The solicitor is correct, counselor. You must think these good jurymen to be imbeciles. Either you make your case on the basis of guilt or on innocence. You will not further confuse the court with your groundless theories. No more mind games, Mr. Heath. Now wrap up your questioning."

"My point here, your honor, is that my client has no guilt because of her mental infirmities acquired as a girl which manifested more deeply as she grew into a young woman."

Judge Bay then spoke in turn. "That reasoning will not work in this court. There is no precedent or case law on the books in this state that sets a body free for reason of insanity. I presume that is the direction you are going. You are not a physician and thus are incapable of providing an expert opinion on such matters."

Heath positioned himself in front of the bench. "You are correct, sir. I am not. But Dr. Jervis Stevens is. And a noted theorist in the area of mental infirmities and dementia as well. I will call him to the stand."

"Your honor. Does counsel wish to deny me an opportunity to question his client?" asked Hayne.

"Go ahead, Mr. Hayne." Harriman cast a depreciative glance in Heath's direction.

"On second thought, your honor. I will not waste my time with her. She already admits her guilt and there is nothing more to explore. But I reserve the right for cross-examination."

"Then return to your chair, Mrs. Fisher. Constable? The court will recess for twenty minutes." Harriman then chuckled. "Nature calls."

CHAPTER TWELVE

3:20 PM

Heath sat at the table, peering over the diary until the *all rise* command was given. When the court was told to sit down, he remained standing. "Your honor, I call Dr. Jervis Stevens."

"Dr. Stevens, please retake the stand," said Harriman. "You are still under oath, sir."

Stevens, looking somewhat puzzled about being recalled, nodded and proceeded to the witness box.

Heath began. "Dr. Stevens, we know you in this community as a respected physician and coroner. We are indeed fortunate to have the services of one of the best educated medical men in our state, if not the country…."

"So much for the adoration, counselor. Now get on with the questioning," Harriman bellowed.

"Where did you get your degree, doctor?"

"My college was William and Mary, sir. Then I graduated from the Harvard Medical School with specialties in Forensics and brain functions."

"Splendid, Dr. Stevens. You have reviewed Mrs. Fisher's case and had personal dialogue with her. Do you have an opinion as to what could have compelled this woman to commit these murderous acts?"

"I must object, your honor," said Hayne, jumping to his feet. "I object to this witness and to any opinions he may have on the woman. He is a medical doctor, and we all agree he is competent in treating physical maladies. Is he also a mind reader or so well versed on satanic matters that he can examine the evil that lays on this woman's black heart?"

"Judge Bay, sir," injected Dr. Stevens. "I have studied in Austria and hypothesized with more famous physicians than me on the mental failings. We have completed many studies, rendering collective opinions as to why even normal people's minds are affected by circumstances and events in our world that cause them to behave in destructive ways. The science of the mind will one day be as recognized and probed just as we do the science of the body."

"Your honor. Please. This is all a ploy. Does the good doctor insinuate that the accused was insane or demented in some way, causing her to murder these poor men? Does he further claim she was not responsible for these heinous acts due to her mental infirmities?"

"Mr. Hayne will have an opportunity to question this witness, your honor," replied Heath. "But now that he has opened this door, I will continue on this route. Doctor, are you saying Lavinia Fisher did not have the capacity to choose right versus wrong, good over evil?"

"I would not go so far as to say that, but I will say there are hurts, if you will, that may materialize in one's childhood that could affect the ability for an otherwise sane and normal person to commit acts against humanity. This does not mean there are demons inhabiting one's soul or that one can clearly be labeled as a criminal or monster. Events and circumstances may serve to depress one's spirit, causing an injury to the mind, much as one's body is injured. As the body may become crippled from an external event upon it, so can the mind become crippled to a point where that person acts beyond his capacity to reason and understand appropriate behavior."

"Thank you, doctor. In your opinion, was Mrs. Fisher incapable of making appropriate decisions, based on her childhood sufferings?"

"Quite possibly, sir. But one has no real way of knowing without an in-depth assessment and perhaps an administration of medicines. There has been some discussion of a medicine extracted from the Venutier Balm plant that grows in Argentina...."

As Dr. Stevens continued his scientific explanation, Heath sensed he was beginning to ramble and did not want the physician's credibility to be in question. "That's good, doctor. I believe you have informed us all very well and I thank you for your testimony. Your witness, Mr. Hayne."

"Now doctor," Hayne began. "This is all very interesting, but there is no exact science established by your medical association that specifically addresses these so-called mental infirmities. Am I correct?"

"There is no exact science, sir, but..."

"But nothing, Doctor Stevens. You have not convinced the court that this woman was insane, possessed, or otherwise mentally incompetent so as to escape responsibility for her grievous crimes. She's evil, doctor. She's nothing but a murderess, driven and consumed by greed." Hayne then turned to the jury. "Mr. Heath here will try any magic, including having you believe in some kind of mental science, to save his client from the gallows."

"Objection!" yelled Heath. "Counselor demeans this witness, a well-respected physician. Furthermore, as he accused me of doing, he now offers a summation of his own. Again, the court is prejudiced with reference to the gallows."

Judge Bay opened his mouth to answer the objection, but Harriman stood from his chair. "Sit down, Mister Heath. You do not tell us what prejudices this court. *We* make such observations. But the prosecutor is correct. I see no evidence produced in this testimony that proves Lavinia Fisher was incapable of choice due to some mental infirmity. If you have finished with your examination, Mr. Hayne, I will excuse the witness."

Heath's face reddened. "I protest your making of such ruling on the testimony, your honor. This is a matter for the jury to determine."

"I will determine the validity of a witness's testimony, counselor."

"I beg to disagree, your honor. You circumvent the process in doing so."

"Again, sit down, Mister Heath. You of all people will not school me on legal decorum. We have the power to decide this woman's fate, along with her conspirators, even without a jury. There is nothing presented by you or Doctor Stevens that convinces me that she should not pay with her life."

Judge Bay placed his hand on Harriman's arm to indicate perhaps he was getting too emotional and had gone too far.

Heath continued. "Then what, pray tell, was the purpose of this trial, if your mind is so set?"

"Take your seat or I will have you placed in irons, counselor!"

Heath plopped contemptuously into his chair, then looked over his shoulder at Matthew Cowher. The minister's lips had tightened and his head dropped sharply into his chest. Peripherally, Heath noticed Lavinia rising slowly from her chair, fists clenched. With venomous eyes cemented on Harriman, she pointed a frail finger in his direction.

"Then you should also pay for your crime, hypocrite. Was it not a crime for you to force yourself into my cell and between my legs? Mrs. Cleary should have shot you where you lay. It would have been worth the taste of your blood on my face had she scattered your brains with her pistol."

Mouths were agape as the entire gallery gasped. Hayne and Bay included. Matthew's chest burned with anger when he heard the charge. Margaret Cleary sat stoically as the eyes of the courtroom finally diverted to her. But it was Harriman who bounded from his chair, smashing and breaking his gavel onto the bench, shouting "Insolent bitch! Mister Heath, I find you responsible for her lying and blasphemous tongue. Either quiet her or you will find yourself in a cell next to hers!"

Judge Bay, now fully facing Harriman, whispered what appeared to be animated admonishment. The entire courtroom buzzed feverishly. Some stood, including Matthew, casting accusatory eyes toward the magistrate. This compelled Harriman to rap on the bench again, but this time with the severed head of the gavel. "Sit down and be quiet, the lot of you! You defile this court. If you do not be still, you will all be removed. Cleary! Bailiff! Do your duties!"

Colonel Cleary stood and turned toward the observers. When he put up his hand, the noise immediately quelled. As if by silent command, they sat down. All except one man. Matthew Cowher raised his arm and with his right index finger, that may as well have been a pistol, pointed to Harriman.

"No! It is you, sir. It is you who defiles this court. You are a bully and a tyrant, and if you did set upon this woman in her cell, it will be my passion from this day forth to see you removed from this bench."

Bay, seeing his courtroom out of control, rapped his gavel. "Please sit now, Reverend Cowher. You are out of order."

Harriman arrogantly leaned forward, fists resting on his bench. Calmly, he reiterated Bay's order, "If you do not sit down, minister, you will be removed. It is only out of respect for the cloth that I do not have you publicly flogged. Take him from the courtroom, Cleary."

Matthew held up his hand to the chief constable and left on his own. Hayne watched him leave, then turned his attention back to Harriman. As he was not only trial counsel but also the attorney general, he set about to distance himself from the madman. His face now revealing great disdain for the magistrate, he asked to speak to Judge Bay in private chambers. The court took a short recess, and as Harriman was not included in the caucus, he sat at the bench, fuming. Judge Bay returned to the courtroom after a few minutes and took the magistrate back into chambers for the better part of an hour. When Bay returned, Harriman was not with him.

As the atmosphere of the room was eventually restored to civility, Judge Bay asked Hayne if he had more evidence to present. "The prosecution rests, your honor."

"Very well. Summations, gentlemen."

The prosecution and defense summations were comparatively less climactic, considering the fireworks of the afternoon. Hayne's eloquent oratory was matter-of-fact and without the earlier swagger and drama. He concluded his fifteen-minute soliloquy by saying, "Gentleman, you have Mrs. Fisher's own admission of these murders, and such testimony leaves the lying co-conspirators with no defense or credibility. From their graves these good dead men cry out for justice. There is only one verdict that you can bring in for each of the accused: guilty!"

Heath re-stated Dr. Stevens' mental infirmity theory to the court and appealed to the jury to consider Lavinia's traumatic history. "A terrible childhood fate has all but slain the rational mind of this unfortunate woman, surely exculpating her from all guilt and blame for these horrific crimes. A sane and logical being would never plot such things. Should she be held accountable for that which lies beyond the mind's control? We mourn the loss of these five wayfarers. They were indeed victims. But consider, as well, so was Lavinia Fisher. I say to you that she is not guilty as she was not of sane mind when she committed her crimes. I give her now to you."

Withrow's summation was equally impassioned. But now that his client had been fully implicated by the confession of Lavinia Fisher, he asked that the court have mercy on John. He could ask for no more under the circumstances.

In less than half an hour, just before five o'clock, the jury reseated themselves on the two benches. William Hart, the foreman, remained standing.

"What say you good men?" asked Bay.

"Your honor," replied Hart, "the jury finds both conspirators guilty."

Mumbling ensued throughout the room. Fisher shook his head, but Lavinia stood expressionless with head and eyes down.

Judge bay polled each juror to assure all are in agreement. He started first with J.S. Packer.

"Guilty."

"Ivan Gespeale."

"Guilty"

"Peter Gaillard"

All of the jurymen stood one by one when their names were called and sounded *guilty*."

The judge then rose from his chair, swept his eyes over the gallery and onto each defendant. Thrusting out his chin in kingly fashion, he spouted with succinct articulation, "Defendants rise for sentencing." He paused to allow them a moment to come to their feet. "I pronounce that you each be hanged by the neck until dead, and to be carried out in the public square on the morning of June second, Eighteen Hundred and Nineteen." The gallery waited for him to add "and may God have mercy on your souls." But he did not.

"Your honor," said Heath, rising. "I will request an appeal on behalf of Lavinia Fisher, as it is not lawful in South Carolina for a married woman or a woman with child to be hanged."

Bay was a bit taken aback at Davey Heath's knowledge of this statute. As a matter of fact, Heath had surprised him during the afternoon with the mental infirmity defense he had put up. The judge took a moment to reflect, wiping his brow thoughtfully with his hand. After a while, he retorted with a surprise of his own. "Well, Mr. Heath, as you seem to have done your homework on this issue, I believe I can provide a solution to this problem. We will first hang the husband, and this will make her a widow. As she will then be an unmarried woman, we will not be breaking the law when we hang her afterward, will we?"

The next day Davey Heath motioned to the Constitutional Court for a new trial, quoting several reasons. First, Harriman's conduct leading into and during the trial was not only reprehensible, but also prejudicial to the case of Lavinia Fisher. Secondly, as a woman had never been hanged in South Carolina, he would challenge the sentencing. The punishment was considered cruel and unusual for a woman. The petition asked for a reversal of the sentencing and that it be instead converted to life imprisonment.

The Constitutional Court of South Carolina immediately stayed the execution until the defense's plea could be taken under advisement. The matter would be argued before the court in January of the next year. The Fishers would live another eight months and see one more Christmas.

CHAPTER THIRTEEN

It was a long, steamy summer for the prisoners. There were times that Lavinia felt she was suffocating from the heat and petitioned the chief constable for a change of cells. "Sir, I lay day after day in this oven drenched in sweat. Even in the night there is no relief."

"I am sorry, Mrs. Fisher. You have one of the lower cells and these are generally the cooler ones. Most of those with windows are unbearably hot. The cells above you and on the top floor are even warmer, and I fear transferring you there will cause you to be even more uncomfortable. I will have Margaret visit you daily with some ice and cool water."

"Thank you for your kindness, Colonel. I must say, of all the officials about the city, I find you the most tolerable. Had I known you before and been on your side of the law, I could see myself as your friend. I do value Margaret's visitations. She is a good woman, although I can often sense the disdain in her voice for my misdeeds."

Cleary nodded. "Even though by your own admission you committed these heinous acts, I still do not wish to see you hanged, madam. Your husband, however, is another matter. I suppose it is my tender heart that influences my head when it comes to the punishment of women. I can't help but believe that your husband had much to do with your committing these miserable acts and had you met up with another, you would not find yourself waiting on the gallows."

Lavinia didn't respond. She knew all too well that it was she who had concocted murder schemes long before John Fisher rode into her life. Beginning with her aunt.

A complement of sixteen ladies, some belonging to the organization called the Christian Women of Charleston, others representing a contingent of women from the Second Independent Unitarian Church, met in the grand home of Minnie Studdard, wife of architect Paul Studdard. Attending the assembly as well were Dr. Richard Furman, pastor of the First Baptist Church, his wife, and the Rev. Matthew Cowher. For nearly an hour, in advance of the meeting, the ladies socialized with one another, whisking about here and there, and preparing platters of short bread, ginger cookies and tea, trying the patience of the men.

Finally, as they all settled in like birds in a tree, poised to engage in chatter, Mrs. Studdard opened the dialogue. "Dr. Furman," she began, "we bring to you our concerns over this whole Fisher woman predicament.

Furman dropped a spoonful of sugar into his cup and raised his head to respond. "Which are, Madam?"

She sighed with great drama. "As to how we women of Charleston will be perceived by the world outside our peninsula. The fact that this woman and her lowly husband have been the talk of our city for the past year, now facing the gallows, indeed reflects derogatorily on every white woman in Charleston. My cousin in New York sent to me an account of this…this indecorous matter, printed in her newspaper. Why it makes it appear that we women of the South are all not only uncultured and profane, but thieves and murderers alike."

Dr. Furman shot a glance in Matthew's direction. There was a glint of jocularity in his eyes. "The article said that?"

Mrs. Studdard cocked her head and looked at the others, then pulled from her sleeve a lace handkerchief to touch each corner of her mouth. "Well…not in so many words. But the tenor of the article made it appear as such."

"I have heard talk as well in Savannah," added Jane Pickerell. "Not ten days ago, I accompanied Mr. Pickerell on one of his buying trips and before a word from my mouth, I was approached by the mayor's wife about Lavinia Fisher and her imminent doom. She asked what heinous crime the woman could have perpetrated to merit the hanging of a white woman. No one ever remembers such a happening in the South, except perhaps to a Negro woman.

Several of the ladies nodded in harmony. One remained stoic, however, refusing to engage in any dialogue. Dr. Furman took notice and put up his hand to hush the others. "My dear Mrs. Cleary. What do you say on the matter?"

"My friends seem to have forgotten that the purpose of our gathering was to consider drafting a petition to the Governor to spare Mrs. Fisher's life. What I hear instead, sir, are concerns about how a white woman's hanging speaks to the world about Charleston womankind and less to do with the issue of humanity. We know the woman deserves to die, but is not our society now more civilized in dealing with a woman's crime than the time of Salem, nearly two hundred years ago? A woman should not be subject to the same barbaric fate as a man, regardless of her crime. Our society compels it, sir. And that is why the woman's life should be spared."

The collective heads nodded again, as though their diluted minds could be manipulated to accept any argument on the matter, depending on which way the wind blew.

"Then, pray tell, Margaret. What do you suggest her fate be?" asked Mrs. Furman.

"That would be entirely to the discretion of Governor Geddes, short of hanging, that is. He could well commute her sentence to life imprisonment. I believe that would suit the people of our city just as well. Hang her husband and the other conspirators, but lock the woman away for life."

Minnie Studdard spoke up again. "I was in the courtroom at her trial and I must say I was most intrigued by Dr. Stevens' discussion of the woman. If we believe her to have been insane, which she certainly had to have been to commit murder as easily as stepping on an ant, then perhaps she should spend all her days in an asylum. A hanging under these circumstances would seem to perpetuate the lesser view the rest of this country has of we Carolinians."

Perhaps the most revered of all the tongues in the group was Sarah Savage, a stanch Unitarian parishioner, who thirty-five years later would be remembered on a wall plaque as "most lofty and rectitude in character." When she spoke, all ears fixated on her soft yet commanding voice.

"May I, Dr. Furman?"

"Of course, Mrs. Savage."

"There is yet another dimension to this matter, besides the concerns of humanity and the reputation of our community. Where is our concern for her immortal soul? Although I am not one of Matthew's Christian believers, I do believe the tenets of the doctrine. His Christ commands us to forgive. Yes, even the Fisher woman. Punish the woman, yes. But whether she lives or dies, her sin must be cast out for the sake of her soul. It is her soul that should be our concern, not seeing to it that her neck is snapped."

It was Sarah who had specifically requested that Matthew attend the meeting, primarily because she knew of his association with Lavinia Fisher. But as passionately as she felt about saving Lavinia from the gallows, she was just as passionate in her respect for Matthew, regardless of their religious differences. And Matthew knew Lavinia Fisher like no one else in the room. Most of the ladies present had come to realize that fact over the past few months and each time Lavinia's name was mentioned, the eyes darted in Matthew's direction. To some, the association did not set well; others in the room just did not know what to make of him and his closeness to the Fisher woman.

To this point, he had remained silent throughout the meeting. But now, after digesting the dialogue, it was his time. "Thank you, Sarah, for bringing up the business of her soul. I implore you ladies to take heed of Sarah's message. I could not have said this any better, even in one of my most rousing sermons. I ask that you pray for the condemned, for her fate, and for her salvation. You do not know her, but I do..."

The heads turned one to the other and whispers broke out.

"...Ahem," he interrupted. "I counseled with her on many occasions when she was a child and even later when she became a young womanhood. And truly, the Evil One has taken his hold on her. But in my counsel, I have found good in her. I have seen her compassion for the downtrodden and I have heard the cry in her voice. A cry even for salvation. But sadly, neither Dr. Furman nor I have been able to bring her to the Father. That does not mean we should not give up our witness for the Almighty. Saving her from a death on the gallows may in fact lead to the saving of her soul and provide through time a genuine contrition. That should be our message to the Governor. Dr. Furman will soon put to pen and paper our plea for the commuting of this death sentence. For whatever reason you do so, I beseech you to affix your signatures to this petition, so that Lavinia Fisher's fate may now be determined by our Governor."

On the 18th of August, Dr. Furman couriered to the Office of the Governor a Petition for Commuting of Sentence for Lavinia Fisher, citing compassionate, religious and humanitarian reasons. Attached to the document were four pages of signatures, mostly women, numbering three-hundred forty-five.

As the summer waned, cellmates John Fisher and Joseph Roberts added even more drama to the anticipatory atmosphere about the city. On September 13th, Roberts sat cross-legged on the plank floor, raising and lowering the large ring to which violent prisoners were often shackled. He was certainly not the dash of a man as was Fisher. Hair long and unkempt and a face broadcasting pockmarks and deep-set, ignoble eyes, Roberts fully looked the part of a criminal. A large scar creased the left temporal area of his head extending to the ear, half of which had been lopped off in a scuffle with the police some years back.

"We will leave soon," said Fisher. "The guard will finish his rounds about seven-thirty and will return to Cleary's office to settle in for the night. Once we push out of here, we'll go over to the livery, find some hemp and take a couple horses. If the mortar around Lavinia's bars is as soft as ours, we'll have no trouble tyin' off a rope and pullin' out that window."

"Won't the deputy hear the commotion?"

"Her cell is on the west side of the jail away from the deputy's earshot. I expect he won't. Anyway, if he does, we'll be long gone before he can get word to the others."

The mortar was indeed soft enough around the iron window frame to allow Fisher and Roberts to dig out and loosen the blocks below the window by pounding in a spoon handle with his boot heel. Once removed, the opening would be conducive for a body to squirt through. As the cell was on the third floor, they would have to shinny down the side of the building while holding onto the makeshift rope fashioned from bedsheets and blankets. One end would be tied off to the floor ring while the other would end just below the second floor. The men would have to drop from there about twelve feet to the ground. Once Lavinia was freed, the prisoners would make their way to the dock and stow away on a cargo vessel, preferably one bound for Cuba.

At seven-forty-five, moments after the deputy had made his final round for the evening, Fisher and Roberts began knotting the sheets and blankets together. Digging out the remainder of the mortar around a hefty block, they waited for the night. At eight-thirty they listened for any sounds of footsteps outside their cell, then pushed out the large block, watching it drop to the earth below. After striking the ground with an audible thud, it cracked in several pieces. First, Roberts squeezed through the hole, grabbed onto the cloth line and lowered himself down the wall, dropping harmlessly to the ground. Fisher followed, but as he hung on the wall near the window of the cell below, a knot pulled loose and he fell, landing on his back. Though he had wrenched his back and sprained his right ankle he was still able to get to his feet and hobble alongside Roberts to the opposite side of the jail to Lavinia's window.

As she had not been privy to the escape plan, Lavinia was asleep on her cot. Fisher rapped hard with a stone on the window bars, prompting her to scream. Constable Worthington who had just made his rounds on the lower level was still in earshot of her cell.

"What's your problem in there?" he yelled, thinking she may have been accosted by a rat. He approached the bars of her cell, held high a lantern and added, "Do we need to set our more traps?" Suddenly there was a second rap on the bars. Worthington drew a pistol from his belt, positioned it through the cell door and pointed it toward the window.

"Get away from the window whoever you are or I'll shoot!" Thinking it may be someone merely taunting the woman, he did not fire. Instead, he figured the presence of the gun and sound of his voice would scare away the trespasser. Seeing the light and hearing the deputy, Fisher and Roberts quickly stepped to either side of the window out of sight.

"You men there!" bellowed another voice, this time from the street. "What are you up to?" It was another constable.

Both men abandoned their mission, ran from the jail yard to the rear of the building in the direction of the dock and escaped into the night. Fisher would have come back later for Lavinia, but he knew their escape would soon be found out and Cleary would summon all the deputies to be vigilant.

The next morning the chief constable sent word to the police authority in neighboring jurisdictions that Fisher and Roberts had escaped. Harriman could not wait for the sun to peek over the city's roofline to visit Cleary at the jail and begin his tirade.

"What kind of slipshod operation do you run here, Cleary?" he barked from the doorway. "You not only let civilians solve your cases for you, but you allow condemned murderers to escape. Do the right thing at this moment and resign."

"Magistrate, I wish neither to discuss the matter with you this morning or to see your face. Now kindly leave my office so that I may set about to capture these men."

"See to it, Cleary. But bringing these cutthroats in will not save your job. If I am not successful in seeing to your removal, then I am sure the good citizens of Charleston will be. The Governor's office will hear of this as soon as my courier reaches Columbia."

Cleary turned his head from the magistrate and with hands folded at the small of his back he walked to the window. "Leave now, Mr. Harriman, and do what you must do. We have nothing more to discuss."

Governor John Geddes did hear of the escape the next morning and posted a $500 reward on their heads. This prompted over a hundred citizens to probe every shack, carriage house, and chicken coop in and around the city, storming the houses of suspected Fisher gang members as well.

Fisher and Roberts had managed to evade roving patrols and vigilantes by hiding in an abandoned stable house near the dock. Roberts wanted to steal a boat and row out after dark to board a schooner in the offshore waters. Fisher, however, resisted, vowing that he would never leave Charleston without Lavinia. The plan was to lay low for a few days, set fire to several buildings well away from the jail as a ruse, then spring Lavinia while constables and citizens alike tried to save their town.

On the night of the fifteenth, however, the escapees, tired, hungry and desperate, entered John Bull's store near the dock just before closing. As the two rummaged through the cheese and fruit bins, Bull slipped out the back door and flagged down a passing constable. Fisher and Roberts, seeing the approaching officer, made off with their foodstuffs and pockets of jewelry and disappeared over the dock at Tradd Street into the chilling waters. Two other officers joined in the pursuit and fired volleys from their pistols in their direction, hitting a small boat under which Fisher and Roberts had sought shelter. With mission lost and survival in question, the men wobbled feebly out of the drink and onto the rocks below the battery. Within forty-eight hours of their escape, they were back in jail. This time in reinforced cells with no window and shackled to a floor ring.

Ironically, the next day, William Heyward, who had jumped bail, was spotted in Columbia, captured, and thrown into the cell next to his friends. "Fisher!" he yelled. "I heared you could have gotten clean away the other night, but you stayed back hopin'to spring your woman. I told you she was trouble. You shoulda give her up years ago."

"Shut up, Heyward! If your woman, Elizabeth, was worth a pile of dog manure, you would have done the same for her. At least my wife does not have the face of a basset hound."

Heyward spat on the floor and said nothing in retort. What could he say? Elizabeth was *indeed* not a pretty woman.

On a gray day in November Harriman's carriage pulled up to the gate of the Old Jail with Marcus at the reins. When the magistrate disappeared through the doorway that led to the chief's office, Marcus walked around to the west side of the building and plopped wearily against the spiny trunk of a large palmetto. From his pocket he took a large green apple and raised it to his mouth to take a huge, crisp chomp. Through the barred window facing him he saw the wanly face of a woman. She did not move or say a word, but fastened her eyes on his. This unnerved Marcus a little and he gathered himself up. They both stood for a while just looking at one another, then Marcus walked toward her slowly and with hesitance like an unsure puppy. When he was within ten feet of the window, he stopped.

"You can come closer. I won't bite you," she said.

"Yes, ma'am." He then held up the apple. "Are you hungry?"

"I have had no appetite for months. Thanks anyway."

"You're her, aintcha?"

Lavinia didn't answer.

"I heerd about you. You're the one what kilt all them men."

"If that's what you've heard, so be it. Are you afraid of me?"

"No. No, ma'am."

She moved closer and placed her fingers around the bars. "You can drop the ma'am and call me Lavinia. It will be comfortable for you to say my name."

"Yes, ma'am…Lavinia. I'm Marcus. Marcus Washington."

"You're the magistrate's man, aren't you?"

Marcus dropped his head and shuffled his feet.

She winced. "I didn't mean that like it sounded. No man should be any other person's man. But you work for Harriman, don't you?"

"I'm his slave. But I'll never be his man."

Neither said anything for a few moments. Then Lavinia began. "What do you think of me, Marcus? Do you see me as a monster like everyone else?"

"You don't look like no monster to me." He smiled just a little. "I ain't in any position to judge you, ma'am…er, Lavinia. I don't know why you did those things and it ain't none o' my business. I s'pose you had your reasons."

Lavinia's face said as much, but she didn't respond.

Marcus continued. "I feel sometimes…like I could take a man's life. Wouldn't do it without reason, though; but sometimes I get mad, Miss Lavinia. It ain't right for anyone to own another human. 'Bout once a day I feel like I could hurt someone…real bad."

Lavinia nodded and pushed her hand through the bars. Marcus appeared stunned, even bewildered, but before his hand touched hers he wiped it on his shirt as though it was unclean. Suddenly, the one voice Marcus loathed to hear bellowed from the front of the Old Jail. "Marcus, you black ass, get away from that window!" In his hand was the buggy whip. "Do I need cut the blood from your back? And you! Dead woman! You have no business with my darkey. Put your hand back inside or I will have that worthless Cleary place you in irons until such time we slip the noose around your neck."

Lavinia glared at him for a moment, then spat in his direction.

Harriman nodded sardonically. "I will anticipate the day that I take my morning piss on your grave, devil girl." With that, he swatted Marcus on the arm with the whip. Marcus didn't as much flinch from its sting, but forged straight ahead without looking at his owner. The magistrate continued barking. "Move it along, imbecile. Your bitch prepares my dinner as we speak."

A DAY OF THANKSGIVING

Cleary House

To Nathaniel Cleary's right sat Margaret, and across from her, Miller, the bachelor. Matthew was at the other end of the table and to his right was the lovely Lady Miranda Flaherty. This was not really Margaret's idea of a set up, but just the same, she wanted her friend to meet the handsome minister. Matthew was dressed in a stately thigh-length black coat, puffy sleeved shirt with a high neck collar and a four-in-hand knotted necktie pulled together into a dignified bow. Nathaniel, wearing his finest gabardine coat and looking equally as dashing, displayed the most gracious of table manners and dialogue.

The ladies, elegantly and impeccably coifed, whose richly colored garments were of the latest design, sat with hands folded in their laps awaiting the minister's blessing.

And so Matthew began:

"Most glorious Heavenly Father, Creator of our universe, we are truly grateful for this bounty You have supplied at our friend's table. We welcome You in our midst with humble and thankful hearts. So often we take Thy daily bread for granted and fail to understand and appreciate that even the least of our needs is so faithfully provided. Bless this home and the gracious hosts who open it to us for the sharing of food and friendship.

"Bless especially those in unfortunate circumstances who by fate or their own choice have fallen from your grace, poor in spirit, and finding but few and meager morsels before them on this day of Thanksgiving..."

Cleary opened one eye to the minister.

"…May our physical strength be nourished, our spirits revived and our joy restored. May we never lose our focus on You and on the living Christ. For it is by Your holy example that we place upon one another our deeds of lovingkindness. In the name of Your blessed Son I pray. Amen."

As Margaret stood to pass around platters of turkey, corn, and potatoes to the right and then the left, Matthew glanced quickly on several occasions at Miranda. She was fair in complexion with high, shapely cheekbones and naturally curly black hair. A most lovely Irish lass perhaps twenty-two or three. She caught his look and his eyes darted away yet another time.

"Sir, do you find me familiar? I find your eyes upon me as though you know me."

Matthew was fully embarrassed and he felt his face flush. He laid his napkin down and bowed slightly from his sitting position. "My apologies, Miss Flaherty. I do not mean to stare. It is just that I find you…"

"Beautiful?" piped Margaret with a smile.

"Margaret," chided her husband.

"Oh, Nate. I was just finishing what Matthew could not. He knows our friend is a beautiful woman. And do you know, Matthew, that she is Tom Flaherty's daughter, freshly here from Ireland?"

"I did not know Tom had a daughter."

"My father came here nearly five years ago after my mum passed. I chose to stay in Londonderry and teach children. But I did miss Father so, and decided to make my home here with him."

"And we are so pleased that you did, my dear," said Margaret, patting her hand.

Matthew ate very little and just picked at his food. Margaret noticed. "Is the dinner not to your liking, Matthew?"

"Yes. Yes, it is excellent, Margaret." He hoped his lack of indulgence had not been construed as finding it distasteful. "It is perhaps the best food I have had in quite some time. It's just that my appetite has suffered lately."

Miller continued to stuff his jowls, but chimed in between shovels. "Could it be because of the Fisher woman, minister?"

Cleary shot him a hot glare. Miller stopped chewing and brought his napkin to his mouth, seemingly to wipe away the errant words that had spilled out.

"Who is this woman of whom you speak, Mr. Miller?"

"Probably said enough, ma'am," he replied.

"Nobody." responded Margaret. "We do not speak of such women in this house. This is a day for Thanksgiving and we do not mention one who shatters the laws of God and man."

Cleary cocked his head toward his wife. "Now, Margaret. Our guest is just inquisitive and it would be rude of us to bring to the table any topic of conversation and leave her in confusion."

It was Matthew's turn for a comment and to put a cap on the discussion. "Miss Flaherty, the woman of whom they speak is a prisoner in Nathaniel's jail awaiting her fate. I have known and ministered to the woman since she was a child, but unfortunately she went the way of the world. What Mr. Miller is alluding to is that she has been my friend of sorts and I have failed her."

"Rubbish," said Margaret. "There are some people who were born of the Devil, and neither God nor his disciples can save them. Matthew, you did your best with the girl, and no man can fault you."

Matthew displayed an uneasiness by readjusting his frame in his chair and scratching his neck. He found Miranda's eyes on his. "What was her crime?" she asked.

The table was silent for a moment, then Miller answered the question. "Murder. Murder and robbery."

Miranda gasped and placed her napkin to her lips.

Margaret jumped up and began clearing the plates away. "No more of this subject, gentlemen. Nathaniel, I'm sure you have smokes and brandy for the men. The veranda awaits. And Mr. Miller, before you leave, I will prepare you a leftover platter. As you have no woman at home to feed you, I will not have you hungry this evening."

"Yes, ma'am. Thank you. I shall look forward to more of this fine dinner."

"And Mr. Miller. On your way home, take a plate of food to the Fisher woman as well."

She looked toward Matthew and her eyes softened. Nathaniel who had moved in behind her kissed the nape of her neck. "You are a good and compassionate woman, my dear. And a wonderful cook."

Matthew decided not to visit Lavinia again as he was once again chastised for his befriending the murderess at the jail. This time it was the ailing senior pastor, Anthony Forster. Instead, Matthew sat before the fire in his office and penned an entry in his journal:

I prayed again today for her soul. Her agnosticism, her blasphemy, her very condemnation of the Almighty alone is criminal enough. But these insanely callused deeds cannot go unpunished. If I had the power to snatch her from the serrated jaws of death even at the expense of losing my revered position, I would gladly give up everything I hold most dear. I do not know what it is I feel in my heart for her. Perhaps it is pity; but pity and charity are love, are they not? If it is love I have felt for her all these years, then I have undermined the very core of my faith. How it is possible that such a heart as hers can be both black and white is beyond my understanding. I know there is goodness in her. The way she goes on about the black people, the genuine love and empathy that she has for the under-trodden and less fortunate, the tenderness in her eyes and touch. . .But she is a living paradox in this world, given to profane outbursts one moment and in soft, poetic voice the next. How can there be two people living inside her? If there had only been some way to exorcise the living devil out of her to make room for the good in her to flourish. . .

He never mentioned her name in any of his writings. But they who would find Matthew's journal after his death would surely recognize Lavinia's face upon those pages.

Christmas Day, 1819

Missing the striking figure of Matthew Cowher standing mournfully at her cell door these months, Lavinia was compelled to spill her soul onto parchment as well. Nathaniel Cleary had allowed her a pen and inkbottle, but it was *he* who stood watch outside her cell while she wrote. But that was all right. He had been kind to her and if she could not be near John or Matthew, Colonel Cleary would do. She longed for her journal, her friend. But someone else had it. Maybe Matthew. Maybe Davey.

The days drag on like slow dripping molasses. The seconds on the hour are unmercifully torturous. I no longer have any concept of time. I see the light streaming through my window each morning and a year passes until it is dark. If I could find it in my soul to pray, I would ask for a release from this day on day suffering. I have spoken twice to John since he tried to escape. I am grateful to Colonel Cleary for the opportunity. We talked about the inevitable and John says that if there were any way he could hang for the both of us, he would hang twice to spare my life. He has been greatly affected by Reverend Furman and says he is now repented of his sins. I suppose I am one of those sins for which he wants forgiven. He was only a petty thief before I came into his life. There was nothing he had done that would hang him. Now he will die because of me.

I stand at the bars of my window and look at the Africans working around their jail. I fully believe I deserve any punishment that comes to me, but those poor miserable creatures bearing the stripes and welts of the devil whip do not.

Oh, if only Reverend Furman could convince the Governor to pardon me. But if I were freed, where would I go? Who would I be?

Where are you, Matthew?

On January 18, 1820, the Reverend Anthony Forster died from pneumonia complications. As Matthew had already taken hold of the reins during the senior pastor's long illness, this did not present to him a particular challenge. However, as he did not feel worthy in assuming pastorship, he would decline any offers by the pulpit committee or hierarchical board. Instead, the young, Most Reverend Calvin Dandridge would be appointed as the Unitarian Church senior pastor.

On the 24th the Constitutional Court convened, and upon careful consonance with his panel of judges, Federal Judge Charles Colcock struck down Heath's motion for a new trial. The Fishers would hang on February 4. And even after six months, there was still no response to the petition by the Governor's office in Columbia.

Again, both Richard Furman and Matthew Cowher appealed to the Constitutional Court for a stay of execution as the Fishers "implored an opportunity for repentance" and asked for time to "meet with their God." The week of February 4 was also race week in Charleston. A celebrated hanging would certainly overshadow the pageantry and excitement of the festivities. The celebrity racehorses, Beggar Girl, Envoy and Corvisart, the beautiful chestnut gelding, must not be upstaged. At the urging of the townsfolk, Harriman reluctantly agreed to postpone the hangings until February 18. But it wasn't his intent to give the Fishers their spiritual time. He made that clear.

When she did sleep, she dreamt often of her family. Although she could not always make out their faces, she knew it was them. She didn't remember much about her father except that he was a farmer in his native Ireland. Having made little more than a meager living, he sold his home in the rural township of Collier and set out with his young bride to seek a better life in America. Lavinia remembered him as a stern man with a dark, full head of hair and a slightly ruddy face. She never knew if that was just his complexion or perpetual sunburn from his toil in the field.

Her mother was smallish, sweet of face and always wearing her hair in pin-up style whether she had donned her finest clothing at Sunday Mass or was in her garden, pruning her luscious red *Firenza* roses.

Lavinia's favorite times were when she sat cross-legged on the plank floor of the veranda, coddling her rag doll and listening to her mother read aloud from Jane Austen's *Sense and Sensibility.* The six-year-old didn't understand some of the words and much of the dialogue, but her mother's soft, melodic voice came out like a song. She could make a story of dramatic passion sound like a fairy tale. It was all very serene and comfortable, those times. The cool spring breeze off the Ashley would catch a hint of jasmine on the vine at the base of the veranda, filling her nostrils with the scent of some exotic French perfume. All her senses were alive and feeding passionately on nature's sweet dessert.

Winslow, always the prankster, would slip up to the edge of the veranda and ruin her moments of carefree bliss with her mother. He would reach through the dowels of the porch rail and pull her black pigtails. She would screech and her mother would scold him. Off he would run, laughing and pumping his fists in the air, satisfied that he had committed his act of torture on his sister and had pretty much gotten away with it. At least until his mother, remembering the bullying even hours later caught him by the shoulders and shook him.

And then Lavinia awakened from her dream. Her eyes were wet and there was that immense craving in her soul to once again be with her mother and father. And even her pesky brother. The same sun that had painted its radiance on her six-year-old face now mocked and violated her through the bars of her cell window. The early morning mosquitoes and flies had already bitten her, raising itchy welts on her neck and arms.

If she could not have her life back, she preferred to die. And even if she was pardoned in the eleventh hour and John was hanged, would she have any desire to live on? Perhaps she could seek out a life with another, but it would probably be a life of boring decency. Then if the pardon did not come, there were any number of men who would still want her. Handsome dandies. Some would even consider leaving their fat, boring wives for her. After John was gone, someone would come forward and propose. She could be re-married right on the gibbet. The law was still the law. South Carolina would not hang a married woman.

Four days before the scheduled executions, Cleary jailed the city's notorious hangman, Jacques Fremont, a drunken French immigrant, despised for his trade, yet celebrated for a mere thirty seconds or so each time he rid Charleston of its vermin. Nothing more than a rum rat, Fremont, described by the *Free Press* as "resembling more an anatomical preparation than a true and living man", was compelled to be locked up within days of public hangings so that he could soberly discharge his duties. If the executions would go off without a hitch, he would then be paid in full with all the drink he desired, landing him in the backstreet gutters until his services were again required. All the while, he cursed the chief constable for his incarceration and treatment, which reduced him to a status equal with murderers and thieves.

Lavinia sat on the edge of the cot in her cell on the afternoon of the 17th, trying desperately to pray. It seemed there was a wall between her and whoever God was. Was her black soul denying her access to Him? Her brain was void of words, and she felt that if there was a God, He would surely appear in her mind or there within the confines of her cell to offer her comfort and peace. But she could understand how He felt. She had rejected, even cursed Him for so long, why would He waste His time with the likes of her. "Well, if Ye will not make yourself known to me, at least Satan will take me in."

Suddenly, she felt another's presence outside her cell and glanced into the dark corridor. Someone was there all right, watching her, making soft but audible breathing noises as though each breath were labored and pained. She knew it was Matthew. Locking her eyes onto the faint outline, Lavinia did not call out. Two souls, one light, one dark, communicated in unaspirated spirit. Then, as quickly as the shadow had appeared, it was gone. As much as her heart ached for just a word from him, perhaps it was best that he did not spend these last hours giving her counsel and comfort. It would be like salt in her wounds and the anguished night hours would be unbearable. This way she could better prepare her mind to face the death that would come in just a matter of hours.

CHAPTER FOURTEEN

February 18, 1820
Charleston, South Carolina

Just after dawn the Reverend Dr. Furman visited the cells of the condemned to share verses of comfort with them and to offer up a parting prayer for their souls. Fisher, realizing his impending doom, had found religion. As he had fallen to his knees, shaking and weeping, Lavinia sat quietly in her wedding dress on the edge of her cot, hands folded in her lap, and refusing to acknowledge the famous minister. That is unless he had news of a pardon.

Matthew sat in the leather wingback chair in the church office, where he had been since midnight. The long, somnolent hours of prayer and uneasiness had worn down his body and spirit. He could not bring himself to see Lavinia on the final day of her life. He had stood at the base of the stairs in the dark shadows of the dungeon the day before, watching her for over a half an hour, reluctant to bring himself to talk or otherwise minister to her. As she had occasionally cast her eyes in the direction of his invisible form, he knew that she knew he was there.

The sun had yet to make its appearance and most everyone's cheeks were cherry red from the biting cold wind. All in all, though, it would not be a bad day for the citizens of Charleston to see a hanging. It was the day history would be made in South Carolina. A woman would hang, and for years to come, people would boast that they were there to witness the event.

The gallows had been constructed the day before on grounds near the Ashley Bridge on Meeting Street approximately ten blocks from the jail. The crowd that had gathered was even larger than when, in 1792, George Washington visited the city and in 1816, when Andrew Jackson received a hero's welcome for bringing victory to America over the British once again. There were staid merchants, trappers and wagoners in coonskin caps, soldiers from nearby Fort Johnson, Dutch, French and Spanish seamen, race week leftovers, slaves and free Negroes, and school children with their barking dogs. The young girls from Madame Talvande's Academy were not, however. The schoolmistress was one of the more vocal ladies who had come out against Lavinia's hanging.

Fashionably clad women in dresses sporting the new high empire waists touched silk handkerchiefs to their eyes to dab the tears brought on by the cold morning breeze. Twenty years later, at the beginning of the Victorian Era, these women would never be present at a hanging.

There were riffraff present as well. Some who had done business with the Fishers lurked, scanning the crowd to see if anyone would associate them with the killers. Dwellers of the ratruns eyed the more affluent and licked their lips at the thought of picking pockets.

Lavinia had tried to sleep the night before and even dozed for a few minutes until she was awakened by the tickle of a roach crawling across her lips. It added insult to the doom she faced. She sat under her blanket on her cot, rocking for hours. Perhaps it was not only that she was cold- she was a little girl again, maybe four or five, sitting in her mother's arms in the front porch rocker. She was scared. Horribly scared at what waited for her. The truth, the implacable truth, was that she was not as much afraid of dying as she was angry. The mob would see her humbled. Silenced. Pitifully…well, dead. That would be their final ridicule of her, and she hated that.

After an emotionally agonizing night, a spear of light formed through the bars and fell onto the floor. Cleary appeared at her cell door with a cup of coffee and a sweet bun. "Shall I bring you some ham and eggs, Lavinia?"

She shook her head and did not look at him. She did manage to murmur, "Thanks just the same. I will consider the offer of a horse, if you're indeed in such a benevolent mood."

Cleary managed a slight smile. But it was a sad smile.

At eight o'clock the prisoners were finally loaded by Cleary and three deputies onto a wagon, shackled to the clapboard and paraded slowly down Meeting toward the north end of the city. When the doomed couple arrived at the gibbet, a roar went up from the surging wave of people. Wicked shouts of scorn and rebuke filled the air, mostly directed at Lavinia. For such a genteel society, public hangings brought out a callousness and barbarism in otherwise pious and civil hearts that, when summoned, collectively created a kind of mob mentality.

As the prisoners were unloaded from the wagon, two policemen held pistols in their right hands and the arm of a condemned in their left. John Fisher's knees weakened and he had to be helped along the path toward the steps of the gallows. Once at the base of the steps, he regained his strength and ascended under his own accord, head down and praying. Lavinia stalled, defiantly. Refusing to place a foot on the bottom step, she became fitful and profane, compelling the deputies to carry her up to the platform. Once both were in place on the gibbet, the hangman positioned them in front of the two-and-a-half-foot boxes under which hung two nooses.

Moving through the crowd, sometimes shoving and bumping men, women and children alike, Matthew Cowher made his way to the base of the scaffold just below Lavinia and beside Dr. Furman. For several moments she and Matthew made unwavering eye contact. Finally, with a half-smile on her face, she turned her eyes to Furman. Barely audible above the chatter of the crowd, she mouthed, "Are you here to tell me the Governor has spared my life?"

Dr. Furman, pale and grim himself, shook his head.

"Then I curse the Governor and you, minister." Her eyes pierced his very soul.

Reverend Furman looked to his right to catch his morose counterpart's reaction. But Matthew did not return the glance. Instead, he stood with head down, left elbow resting on his right wrist tucked tightly into his abdomen, and hand covering most of his face. Dr. Furman took from his pocket a piece of paper on which John Fisher had scribbled a message earlier that morning. After slowly ascending the steps of the gibbet, he placed his eyeglasses on the bridge of his nose and began addressing the blood-hungry mob:

"The man here, John Fisher, has written a letter of sorts to you good citizens of Charleston. In conversing with the condemned, I found him to be remorseful for his deeds as he conveyed to me with a simple tongue. However, Mr. Fisher's pen is surprisingly profound. As it may matter little to you, the content of the letter matters much to the Almighty, and I am compelled to place it upon your ears.

Reverend and Dear Sir,

The appointed day has arrived——the moment soon to come, which will finish my earthly career. It behooves me for the last time to address you and the reverend gentlemen associated in your pious care.

For your exertions in explaining the mysteries of our Holy religion and the merits of our Dear Redeemer, for pious sympathy and benevolent regards as concerned our immortal souls, accept, Sir, for yourself and them the last benediction of the unfortunate. God in His infinite mercy, reward you all.

In a few moments, the world to me shall have passed away. Before the throne of the Eternal Majesty of Heaven, I must stand. Shall then at this dreadful hour my convulsed, agitated lips still proclaim a falsehood? No! Then by that Awful Majesty I swear I am innocent. May the Redeemer of the world plead for those who have sworn away my life.

To the unfortunate, the voice of condolence is sweet, the language of commiseration delightful, these feelings I have experienced in the society of the Reverend Cowher. . . .

Matthew lifted his head to meet Fisher's eyes. He had tried to counsel with him several times to no avail, detecting the man's jealousy. Had Fisher, after all, allowed Matthew's witnessing for the Lord God to penetrate his black soul? Matthew then looked at Lavinia, who stood expressionless. Those words. Those eloquent words were none other than hers. For it was she who had the gift of words. . .words from the very bosom of Robert Burns. But did this mean she had finally embraced God's mercy and love? If so, why then did her behavior contradict the words? And why did she give the words to John, signing his name? Was she still too proud to confess her sins with her own pen?

Furman continued:

. . .A friend, he rejected not our prayer. He shut not his ear to our supplication. He has alleviated our sorrows. He has wept with us. May God bless him. May angels rejoice with him. He deserted me not in this life. To him I bid farewell. . .

As the statement came to a close, Matthew had long since returned his eyes to the soil beneath his feet. He was both saddened and embarrassed, as all eyes were now upon him.

Dr. Furman folded the paper and removed his spectacles. "Mr. Fisher, do you wish to add to these words?"

"I tell you today, I am innocent of these crimes. It was Colonel Cleary who spoke my name to the man, Peeples. It was he who put notions into the man's head so as to enable him to identify me. My blood is on Colonel Cleary's hands."

Cleary stared in stony silence at Fisher, eyes bearing down on him and hands formed in military fashion behind his back. Fisher's prayer before the Almighty meant nothing if he could not with his mouth confess his guilt and sin before those who would soon witness his death.

Within moments at the nod of Chauncey Harriman, the crier took center stage. "Hear ye! Hear ye!" Before you, stand two condemned murderers who having been found guilty of crimes against humanity shall pay the price for their terrible deeds and hang by their necks until they are dead! May God have mercy upon their poor souls!"

Harriman, perched atop the broad cow pony that supported his large frame, resembled a victorious king overseeing subjects following his ruling of execution. The breakfast of eggs, scrapple and biscuits was already gurgling in his stomach, so with a commanding expression on his face aimed at Cleary, he motioned with a twirl of his hand for him to quickly proceed with the first execution.

Fisher turned to his wife. "Lavinia, I have loved you from the first day I laid eyes on you. I don't know where we're goin' after this, but wherever it is, we'll get there at the same time." He turned his face back to the crowd and closed his eyes as if in prayer.

Lavinia bit her lip as the hangman placed the hood over John's head. When she turned her head back toward the crowd, she heard the thud of the hangman's boot against the box, followed by the snap of her husband's neck. His legs pawed aimlessly in the air for a place to support the choking body. After a few seconds the body relaxed, rocking lazily back and forth like a child on a rope tree swing. As the crowd roared with approval, Lavinia remained emotionless and unflinching. The despised hangman, who had the ultimate power to carry out sentences of judges, had done so with glee. His was the job no one else would do. At that moment he was indeed the most powerful yet scorned man in Charleston. When this was all done, however, he would again become a drunken nobody until the day his work was needed again.

Now the mob that had assembled in such number to witness the next hanging suddenly became silent. Charleston had seen many an execution of pirates, slaves and murderers, but were they really prepared to see a woman swing from the rope?

Cleary approached her, appearing somewhat uneasy, even reluctant. Perhaps it was not just because she was a woman. He had gotten to know her these months and since it was he and Margaret who had rescued her from being ravaged by the despicable Harriman, that experience had given them a degree of association. But she was still a murderess, several times over, and he was bound to carry out his duty.

"Lavinia Fisher, do you have a final request?" he asked.

She nodded to him, then took the two or three steps to the hanging body of her dead husband. "Would you be so kind as to remove his hood, Colonel Cleary?"

Although a bit puzzled, he did as she requested. Fisher's face was blue and distorted. His sorrowful eyes, still open and cast downward, were cemented in a glossy gaze as though he was concentrating on the large woman in the blue dress two rows deep. The woman, receiving his death stare, gasped with the sound of a woodthrush and turned away quickly. Lavinia moved the box toward her dead husband with her foot, gingerly stepped upon it and kissed him. A hush went over the crowd. "My John. Dear John. Your lips are still warm, even though death's wing has overtaken you. Goodbye. I will look for you in Hell's blazing furnace."

She then stepped down and asked Cleary if she could address the crowd. He nodded. The faces were transfixed on hers in anticipation. Her voice was small in the courtyard, like a whisper in a storm. But the sudden silence of the mob straining to hear that voice, still sensuous but cracking with emotion, allowed her to be heard. "Is there a man here who will now be my husband? If you will marry me now, my life will be spared. As you see, I have dressed for either a wedding or my hanging. Which will it be?"

The gallery was stunned. As her eyes continued to scan the congregation, she saw men talking among themselves, some laughing, some with puzzled expressions, but no one responded. If she had not been a condemned murderess, a hundred men would have thrown themselves at the feet of this beautiful woman. She did not look toward Matthew, however. Even to save her neck, she would not disrespect this man or defile his reputation by posing the offer to him. It seemed that minutes had passed while she waited for even one voice to shout "I will." But there was only now an unholy silence.

"Get on with this, Colonel Cleary!" Harriman shouted from his horse. "Dispense from this nonsense."

Lavinia stepped back and onto the block without a coaxing from Cleary. Looking over the crowd, she balled up her fists, shouted obscenities and stomped her foot in contempt. As the hangman approached her to put the rope around her neck, she said, "To Hell with you bitches and sons of bitches. Go ahead and take a look at me. Take a *good* look. That's what you came to see, isn't it? But if any of you has a message for the devil, then tell it to me now, for I will see him this very day." With blue eyes burning into the crowd and lips curled in harvested wrath, she added "But bear righteous witness. The grave will not hold my spirit. I will return to take revenge on this entire city. You will find my hand in every tragedy and ill deed that befalls you."

When it appeared she had said her last, the hangman approached her with intent to place her onto the box. She then turned to him and shrieked "Get away from me, imbecile. I will not give you the satisfaction of hanging me." With that said, she stepped into the noose herself and jumped off the box. Matthew turned his head quickly to the side and closed his eyes. Some dozen streets over, St. Michael's sounded. The hammer now upon the matin bell chimed nine times as if to signal the final fateful stroke of death.

The crowd of onlookers who had earlier shouted "murderess" and "hang the woman" and who had come to celebrate the ending of her life, fell into a hush. The sight of a woman in a wedding dress, head fallen askew and a beautiful face now distorted in death, quelled their cheers. Some stood with mouths agape, some with heads down, and others just walked away without word. A few adults, realizing the grotesqueness of the event and chiding themselves for bringing their young darlings, whisked them away, shielding their eyes from further horror. But one battery rogue, already drunken by nine o'clock, shouted from the rear, "Good show, Lavinia!"

A sudden rush of nausea developed in Matthew's stomach, making him feel feverish and flushed. Bending forward, he placed the palms of his hands on his knees. Dr. Furman, still at his side, placed a cool hand on the back of Matthew's neck and whispered a prayer in his ear. After his *amen* he added "Be strong, my friend." Matthew stood upright again, but refrained from looking in the direction of the dead Lavinia. Cleary, still standing on the gibbet looked down at Matthew. When the two men's eyes met, Cleary shook his head, sadly.

The red winter sun finally managed to peek through the clouds atop the buildings near the east battery, casting its radiance onto the hanging bodies. Its rays caused the white dress to give off an eerie iridescence as though the woman's spirit was still alive and glowing beneath the garment.

Harriman nodded pompously, then turned his horse away and into a trot. The choppy canter of the beast only served to further churn up the garbage in his gut. Home and privy might indeed be too far away.

As Cleary and his officers took down the lifeless forms, Matthew re-donned his hat and turned his eyes toward the rooftops and spires silhouetted against the ever-reddening horizon. Before the day was done, there would be rain. A cold, chilling rain. One that brings on an aching and misery. Much like what he was already feeling in his heart.

CHAPTER FIFTEEN

Epilogue

John Peeples stayed the day to watch the gravediggers plant the coffins that contained the bodies of Charleston's notorious mass murderers in what would become unmarked graves in the Unitarian Cemetery. The next morning, the nineteenth, after assuring the twelve foot deep grave of Lavinia Fisher had not been unearthed, thus allowing her spirit to escape, he mounted his horse and rode west to Georgia. To home and family. Henceforth, ever vigilant in every endeavor of his life, he never again slept in a bed other than his own.

A few days later, the City of Charleston planted an English oak on Lavinia's grave. It was a tree whose massive roots would one day engulf and strangle the coffin of the so-called Mistress of Mayhem. Its powerful tentacles would intertwine and crush what remained of Lavinia Fisher. The white wedding dress would disintegrate into the earth along with the powder of her bones. The oak would serve as a natural monument to the city's triumph over evil.

As there was no one to claim Lavinia's meager belongings, Colonel Cleary bundled them up and dropped them by Matthew's cottage. There was a hairbrush, several tear-stained handkerchiefs, and three books: *Persuasion* and *Pride and Prejudice*, by Jane Austen, and the poems of Robert Burns.

In the late spring of that year, the night sky took on a lurid orange glow to the north of the Ashley Bridge along the Old Dorchester Road where the inn known as Six Mile House ignited in flames. Some say it was set afire by William Hastings' oldest son, who had taken his father's route south from Philadelphia with no other reason but to reduce the notorious inn to ashes. Others say the house fell by God's own hand as lightning from a sudden spring storm struck the roof, setting the place to burn, and releasing the spirits of the murdered souls who had been confined within its evil walls. Nonetheless, the Six Mile Inn had perished. As surely as its mistress had met her tragic end, the batten boards of the stately boarding house lay crumbled in ashen ruins.

In June the grounds were sold in auction for a mere one hundred dollars to a local farmer who had designs on putting in a patch of butter beans near a small family cemetery. Colonel Cleary was again summoned to the property to investigate the discovery of as many as fourteen human remains unearthed by the tiller's blade. Years later when other bones were found in various plots on the premises, it was speculated that as many as twenty-three boarders had perished at the hands of the murderous Fishers over their nine year spree of terror.

After having been tried as well for Hastings' and the others' murders, Heyward was hanged in August.

In late October of that year, Marcus Washington began a search of the house and grounds of the Harriman estate for his wife Kendra. As Mrs. Harriman was on her deathbed, consuming much of Kendra's days, Marcus assumed Kendra had gone out to catch a breath of fresh air or was in the kitchen house, mixing up an elixir Harriman had fetched from the apothecary. As Marcus neared the stable, he heard muffled cries that sounded like a small animal in pain. When he crossed the threshold into the building, to his horror, he saw Harriman humped over Kendra. The fat man had bent her over a small table and hiked her dress high atop her buttocks. She was sobbing bitterly through the fingers of the rapist who had his hand over her mouth attempting to quell her cries. Harriman turned just in time to see the two powerful hands close around his throat like a vice, crushing the windpipe and stopping his heart. He gurgled and his face took on the color of ashen purple. When he had breathed his last, his lifeless body dropped from Marcus' hands onto the dirt floor.

The magistrate's body was found in the stable by a neighbor only minutes later and word was sent to the chief constable. Cleary threw his musket over his saddle and rode out to Harriman's house. He almost felt sorry for the man as he stood over his body. The bulging eyes were still open, his neck crushed and twisted, privates exposed and trousers around his ankles. Not a pretty death scene. There was no doubt that it was Marcus who had killed the magistrate. And considering the way Harriman lay, either Marcus had caught the man violating Kendra or he had finally snapped under the bloodthirsty whip, leaving Harriman strangled and ridiculed in death. But Cleary knew it was not the latter. In checking Marcus' quarters, Cleary found the cabin empty. Marcus, his wife, and two sons had slipped away.

Word came from Miller that someone had spotted Marcus and his family running toward Carter's Landing on the river not more than twenty minutes before. "Shall I get a couple of men and cover the woods in that area, Chief?"

"No. I will take care of this matter myself. Send word to Margaret to look in on Mrs. Harriman. She is all alone now."

Cleary then sprang onto his horse with the agility of a twenty-year-old and accelerated quickly to a gallop toward the Ashley. As he reined in his steed just shy of the tree line at water's edge, he caught sight of the family disappearing into the river oaks. Swinging his leg over the saddle, he secured his musket and dropped to the ground. When he moved stealthily into the woods, Cleary was startled by a covey of quail springing from the marsh, prompting him in reflex to swing his rifle in their direction. By the time the river came into his view, Marcus and his family were in an abandoned rowboat, pushing off from the shore.

As Marcus dipped the oar into the water to take the boat downstream, he noticed his boys staring frightfully back toward the shore. Standing on the bank, stoic and still, with musket raised, was the Chief Constable. Marcus relaxed the oar in the water and fixed his eyes on Cleary. The Chief closed his left eye and cocked the flintlock, placing a bead on the chest of the slave man. Marcus outstretched his arms as if to say "Here I am, sir. Do as you will." Cleary stood for perhaps twenty seconds, poised to fire, and then slowly lowered the rifle. The two men's eyes locked onto one another for several moments. Cleary then nodded once. Marcus stood transfixed for while then retrieved the oar and pushed it slowly through the water. Their stares upon each other remained, unwavering. All the while, Cleary stood expressionless, watching the boat drift steadily toward the middle of the river, then disappear from sight.

A few days later, the word about town was that the slave Marcus had perished with his family in the waters of the Ashley the very night of Harriman's murder. No one actually knew who started the story, and Cleary would neither confirm nor deny its validity. As far as he was concerned, the slave family was dead. But some months later, a local trader told Cleary he was sure he recognized Marcus on a slave block in a Savannah square.

The murmuring among the Charlestonians had already begun. Was the death of Chauncey Harriman an omen that the spirit of the Daughter of Darkness had indeed returned?

Colonel Nathaniel Cleary resigned on December 31st as the City of Charleston's faithful Chief of Constables. No one knew why nor did Cleary ever divulge his reason. Scarcely a month later, he caught a debilitating cold and died suddenly from pneumonia. Although Nathaniel Cleary had been a member of the First Baptist Church, Margaret Cleary asked that his friend of seven years, Matthew Cowher, officiate the service.

Eulogy of Colonel Nathaniel Cleary
First Baptist Church, January 27, 1821

"Comes a man into this world, born of humble stock and remaining humble in character and spirit all his life, so we mourn the death of our beloved brother, Nathaniel Cleary. A man of impeccable moral fiber, he was a friend to most, but respected by all. Colonel Cleary fought with General Jackson to defend and preserve this young country, but we knew him best these few years not only as the defender of our city, but a defender of all people, rich or poor. I never knew a fairer man…a man who was astute in both Constitutional Law and the Holy Scripture, perhaps beyond that of many judges and ministers. And he was a man who lived his life in strict obedience to the tenets of God's and man's laws.

"To you, dear Margaret, I leave you with this…"

Ever poised, ever dignified, quashing the swelling of tears that begged to be released, she lifted her eyes.

"…Nathaniel never spoke with me about any matter unless your name was at some point on his lips. You were his fortress, his daily inspiration, and the one true love in his life. We were all fortunate to have communed with him in this world and we take great comfort in knowing he is at last in the presence of Almighty God."

Matthew reached out to place his hand on the coffin before him and raised his eyes toward the ornate Tracery ceiling. "Sleep in peace, my brother. We shall one-day join you in the singing of praises to God our Father."

The town had all but stopped for three days to mourn their beloved peace officer.

In February of 1822, Matthew wed a high-spirited young woman, twenty years his junior, named Miranda Flaherty, daughter of a longtime Unitarian parishioner. With hair the color of a raven's coat, she was strikingly beautiful. The tongues of society did wag again, however, remarking how closely she resembled "the woman who murdered all those people up at Six Mile House." But the talk did not bother Matthew as his new wife, Miranda Cowher, was helping him heal his festering wounds from the past two years. Moreover, she bore him two beautiful children, a son and a daughter. Matthew would never be the Unitarian senior pastor nor did he ever desire the post. There had been a political underpinning within the church regarding his steadfast Christianity; some members were still endeared to him while others wanted him out. There was also just too much controversy about a minister who had the propensity for witnessing to Africans, derelicts and common riff-raff alike when there were spiritual needs within his own church body. And then there was the talk about his association with that Fisher woman some time back.

Denmark Vesey's slave conspiracy ended April 22, 1822 when his plan to free Charleston's slaves and burn the city to the ground was found out. He, along with Gullah Jack and a band of thirty-five, was captured and shackled to stocks near the marketplace. They were to be hanged without trial the next morning. The Reverend Morris Brown, an African religious leader in the city who spent his life ministering to the slave community, appealed to Judges Bay and Colcock for a trial. But his pleas fell on deaf ears. Before the second largest assembled mob in two years, thirty-seven black men were hanged on the 23rd, one by one. One of these was a tall, muscular man named Marcus Washington.

On February 18, 1850, the Right Reverend Matthew Cowher, now in his seventies and a widower, sat in his old leather wingback, gazing affectionately upon the haunting face of a young beautiful, raven-haired woman whose tempestuously wicked half smile and seductive eyes were so vividly captured by the artist's meticulous hand. In his lap lay the journal of the Mistress of Six Mile, who though commonly educated and barely twenty-seven years of age, penned the compelling prose that conjured up a profound and beautiful sadness in Matthew's heart. Although he had read the words many times over, it seemed as though she had written them only yesterday:

I know they will come for me someday and I will be ready. I must pay the ultimate penance for my sins. My life has little meaning anyway without Matthew. John is a faithful husband, but he does not stir my heart like this righteous man, born from the very fiber of God Himself. I have wanted so desperately to be that child of light, but I was doomed to darkness the day I came into this callused world. Neither God's love nor Matthew's prayers can melt the ice that has formed around my heart. Perhaps it is my pride that keeps me from loving humanity. That same pride will one-day be but a withered core as I sit waiting for my doom. Help me, Matthew. Help me before my mirthless soul finally turns as black as pitch. . .

Matthew sighed. If only she had let him. He moved a smaller log onto a large one with his poker, causing the fire to further enrage and crackle. Slowly closing the pages of the journal, he held it for a moment in front of his face, then dropped it onto the blaze. When the diary finally caught fire, it created a sudden burst of flame that began to devour its contents like a ravenously angry god. Pages curled under the intense heat, then blackened into ash. Matthew gave another heaving sigh and kept his eyes trained on the blaze until the cover disintegrated into unrecognizable remains. As the fire cleansed and purged the words of one tormented soul, so did it warm another's ailing body and spirit on that cold Charleston morning.

Matthew was buried in the Unitarian churchyard alongside elders and parishioners, some of whom he had schooled and converted to Christianity and others who preceded his arrival nearly fifty years before. Not long after midnight on the day he was interred, Solomon Fink, church and grounds caretaker, closed the door to the sanctuary and walked along the stone path toward the gate. As a consuming fog fell across the gravestones, Solomon looked back respectfully toward his friend's grave. Suddenly, the half moon's light filtered by the mist revealed the figure of a beautiful raven-haired woman in a diaphanous, flowing white dress. She turned her face slowly toward his, compelling him to call out to ask her business this late in the churchyard. But something in his throat choked off his voice. The fog then thickened, shutting out the moon's glow.

Solomon took a few steps toward Matthew's grave, holding the lantern high above his head. The figure was still there, eyes impassioned, almost pleading as she stared back at him. Then as quickly as she had appeared, she faded, first into the fog, then into nothing.

"Good God!" he exclaimed.

His feet felt like stones, but Solomon did manage with some apprehension to move closer to the grave. He rubbed his tired, burning eyelids with the tips of his fingers, then lowered the lantern down to the freshly planted earth. There before him was a small silver and ivory object lying within inches of his feet. Solomon leaned down to pick it up, and immediately realized he had seen it before. Maybe thirty years before. As though he had just retrieved a hot ember of coal, he dropped the antique cameo broach back upon Matthew Cowher's grave.

A decade after her grandfather's death, twelve-year old Lavinia Anne Cowher rummaged through an old trunk in the attic and pulled out a soiled and faded book of poems by Robert Burns copywritten in 1801. On the inside cover were the now faintly readable initials, "L.F." As she leafed through the time-yellowed pages of the heirloom, someone had carefully under-lined the poet's words:

One life,
One love.
But I shall remember thee
From one life to the next.
For the memory of the living
Is the dwelling place of the dead.

Matthew's granddaughter continued to peruse the pages until she reached the inside of the back cover. In elegant script was penned these three sentences:

I am never dead as long as my name is on another's lips. But if you must speak of me, be gentle with my name. Try to think kindly of me and dwell not on my deeds, for I am but a lost soul, a child of darkness who has had no place in this world.

Lavinia

Made in the USA
Charleston, SC
01 November 2011